Thomas M. Meine (ed.)

SEVEN HORRIBLE HORROR STORIES

IN THE VAULT
by H.P. Lovecraft (1925)

RATTLE OF BONES
by Robert E. Howard (1929)

THE MONKEY'S PAW
by W.W. Jacobs (1902)

THE GHOST EXTINGUISHER
by Gulett Burgess (1905)

DOOM OF THE HOUSE OF DURYEA
by Earl Peirce Jr. (1936)

THE VOICE OF THE NIGHT
by William Hope Hodgson (1907)

THE PHANTOM REGIMENT OF KILLIECRANKIE
by Elliott O'Donnell (1911)

Bibliographic information published by the Deutsche
Nationalbibliothek: The Deutsche Nationalbibliothek lists this
publication in the Deutsche Nationalbibliografie; detailed
bibliographic data are available on the Internet at http://dnb.dnb.de

Manufactured and published by
BoD – Books on Demand, Norderstedt

April 2024

ISBN 9 783758 301018

Contents

Page

IN THE VAULT
by H. P. Lovecraft (1925)

Dedicated to C. W. Smith, from whose suggestion the central situation is taken.

As I view it, there is nothing more absurd than that conventional association of the homely and the wholesome that seems to pervade the psychology of the multitude. Mention a bucolic Yankee setting, a bungling and thick-fibred village undertaker, and a careless mishap in a tomb, and no average reader can be brought to expect more than a hearty, albeit grotesque, phase of comedy. God knows, though, that the prose tale that George Birch's death permits me to tell, has aspects in it, besides which some of our darkest tragedies are light.

Birch acquired a limitation and changed his business in 1881, yet he never discussed the case when he could avoid it. Neither did his old physician, Dr. Davis, who died years ago.

It was generally stated that the affliction and shock were the results of an unlucky slip whereby Birch had locked himself for nine hours in the receiving tomb of Peck Valley Cemetery, escaping only by crude and disastrous mechanical means. Still, while this much was undoubtedly true, there were other and blacker things that the man used to whisper to me in his drunken delirium toward the end.

He confided in me because I was his doctor and because he probably felt the need to confide in someone else after Davis died. He was a bachelor, wholly without relatives.

Birch, before 1881, had been the village undertaker of Peck Valley, and was a very calloused and primitive specimen, even as such specimens go. The practices I heard attributed to him would be unbelievable today, at least in a city. Even Peck Valley would have shuddered a bit had it known the easy ethics of its mortuary artist in such debatable matters as the ownership of costly 'laying-out' apparel invisible beneath the casket's lid and the degree of dignity to be maintained in posing and adapting the unseen members of lifeless tenants to containers not always calculated with the sublimest accuracy.

Most distinctly, Birch was lax, insensitive, and professionally undesirable, yet I still think he was not an evil man. He was merely crass of fiber and function – and thoughtless, careless, and fond of drinking, as his easily avoidable accident proves, and without that modicum of imagination that holds the average citizen within certain limits fixed by taste.

Just where to begin Birch's story, I can hardly decide, since I am no practiced teller of tales. I suppose one should start in the cold December of 1880, when the ground froze and the cemetery delvers found they could dig no more graves till spring.

Fortunately, the village was small and the death rate low, so it was possible to give all of Birch's inanimate charges a temporary haven in the single antiquated receiving tomb. The undertaker grew doubly lethargic in the bitter weather and seemed to outdo even himself in carelessness.

Never did he knock together flimsier and ungainlier caskets or disregard more flagrantly the needs of the rusty lock on the tomb door, which he slammed open and shut with such nonchalant abandon.

At last, the spring thaw came, and graves were laboriously prepared for the nine silent harvests of the grim reaper that waited in the tomb. Birch, though dreading the bother of removal and interment, began his task of transference one disagreeable April morning but ceased before noon because of heavy rain that seemed to irritate his horse after having laid but one mortal tenement to its permanent rest. That was Darius Peck, the nonagenarian, whose grave was not far from the tomb.

Birch decided that he would begin the next day with little old Matthew Fenner, whose grave was also nearby, but postponed the matter for three days, not getting to work till Good Friday, the 15th. Being without superstition, he did not heed the day at all, though ever afterward he refused to do anything of importance on that fateful sixth day of the week. Certainly, the events of that evening greatly changed George Birch.

It was on the afternoon of Friday, April 15th, when Birch set out for the tomb with horse and wagon to transfer the body of Matthew Fenner.

He subsequently admitted that he was not perfectly sober, though he had, by then, not been taken to wholesale drinking, by which he later tried to forget certain things. He was just dizzy and careless enough to annoy his sensitive horse, which, as he drew it viciously up at the tomb, neighed and pawed, and tossed its head, much as on that former occasion when the rain had vexed it.

The day was clear, but a high wind had sprung up, and Birch was glad to get shelter as he unlocked the iron door and entered the side-hill vault.

Another might not have relished the damp, odorous chamber with the eight carelessly placed coffins, but Birch in those days was insensitive and was concerned only about getting the right coffin for the right grave. He had not forgotten the criticism aroused when Hannah Bixby's relatives, wishing to transport her body to the cemetery in the city where they had moved, found the casket of Judge Capwell beneath her headstone.

The light was dim, but Birch's sight was good, and he did not get Asaph Sawyer's coffin by mistake, although it was very similar. He had, indeed, made that coffin for Matthew Fenner, but had cast it aside at last as too awkward and flimsy, in a fit of curious sentimentality aroused by recalling how kindly and generous the little old man had been to him during his bankruptcy five years before.

He gave old Matt the very best his skill could produce but was thrifty enough to save the rejected specimen and to use it when Asaph Sawyer died of a malignant fever. Sawyer was not a lovable man, and many stories were told of his almost inhuman vindictiveness and tenacious memory for wrongs, real or imagined. To him, Birch had felt no compunction in assigning the carelessly made coffin, which he now pushed out of the way in his quest for the Fenner casket.

It was just as he had recognized old Matt's coffin that the door was slammed shut in the wind, leaving him in a dusk even deeper than before. The narrow transom admitted only the feeblest of rays, and the overhead ventilation funnel virtually none at all, so that he was reduced to profane fumbling as he made his halting way among the long boxes toward the latch.

In this funereal twilight, he rattled the rusty handles, pushed at the iron panels, and wondered why the massive portal had grown so suddenly recalcitrant. In this twilight, too, he began to realize the truth and to shout as if his horse outside could do more than neigh an unsympathetic reply. The long-neglected latch was obviously broken, leaving the careless undertaker trapped in the vault, a victim of his own oversight.

The thing must have happened at about three thirty in the afternoon. Birch, being by temperament phlegmatic and practical, did not shout long but proceeded to grope about for some tools, which he recalled seeing in a corner of the tomb. It is doubtful whether he was touched at all by the horror and exquisite weirdness of his position, but the bald fact of imprisonment so far from the daily paths of men was enough to exasperate him thoroughly.

His day's work was sadly interrupted, and unless chance presently brought some rambler hither, he might have to remain all night or longer.

The pile of tools soon reached, and with a hammer and chisel selected, Birch returned over the coffins to the door. The air had begun to be exceedingly unwholesome, but to this detail he paid no attention as he toiled, half by feeling, at the heavy and corroded metal of the latch.

He would have given much for a lantern or bit of candle, but lacking these, he bungled semi-sightlessly as best he might.

When he perceived that the latch was hopelessly unyielding, at least to such meager tools and under such tenebrous conditions as these, Birch glanced about for other possible points of escape.

The vault had been dug from a hillside, so that the narrow ventilation funnel at the top ran through several feet of earth, making this direction utterly useless to consider.

Over the door, however, the high, slit-like transom in the brick facade gave promise of possible enlargement to a diligent worker. Hence, upon this, his eyes long rested as he racked his brains for means to reach it.

There was nothing like a ladder in the tomb, and the coffin niches on the sides and rear – which Birch seldom took the trouble to use – afforded no ascent to the space above the door. Only the coffins themselves remained as potential stepping stones, and as he considered these, he speculated on the best mode of arranging them. Three coffin heights, he reckoned, would permit him to reach the transom, but he could do better with four.

The boxes were fairly even and could be piled up like blocks, so he began to compute how he might most stably use the eight to rear a scalable platform four deep. As he planned, he could only wish that the units of his contemplated staircase had been more securely made. Whether he had imagination enough to wish they were empty, is strongly to be doubted.

Finally, he decided to lay a base of three parallel with the wall and to place upon this two layers of two each, and upon these a single box to serve as the platform. This arrangement could be ascended with a minimum of awkwardness and would furnish the desired height.

Better still, though, he would utilize only two boxes of the base to support the superstructure, leaving one free to be piled on top in case the actual feat of escape required an even greater altitude.

And so the prisoner toiled in the twilight, heaving the unresponsive remnants of mortality with little ceremony as his miniature Tower of Babel rose, course by course.

Several of the coffins began to split under the stress of handling, and he planned to save the stoutly built casket of little Matthew Fenner for the top so that his feet might have as certain a surface as possible.

In the semi-gloom, he trusted mostly to touch to select the right one, and indeed came upon it almost by accident, since it tumbled into his hands as if through some odd volition after he had unwittingly placed it beside another on the third layer.

The tower at length finished, and his aching arms rested by a pause during which he sat on the bottom step of his grim device. Birch cautiously ascended with his tools and stood abreast of the narrow transom.

The borders of the space were entirely brick, and there seemed little doubt but that he could shortly chisel away enough to allow his body to pass.

As his hammer blows began to fall, the horse outside whinnied in a tone that may have been encouraging and may have been mocking. In either case, it would have been appropriate, for the unexpected tenacity of the easy-looking brickwork was surely a sardonic commentary on the vanity of mortal hopes and the source of a task whose performance deserved every possible stimulus.

Dusk fell and found Birch still toiling. He worked largely by feeling now since newly gathered clouds hid the moon, and though progress was still slow, he felt heartened at the extent of his encroachments on the top and bottom of the aperture. He could, he was sure, get out by midnight, though it is characteristic of him that this thought was untinged with eerie implications.

Undisturbed by oppressive reflections on the time, the place, and the company beneath his feet, he philosophically chipped away the stony brickwork, cursing when a fragment hit him in the face, and laughing when one struck the increasingly excited horse that pawed near the cypress tree.

In time, the hole grew so large that he ventured to try his body in it now and then, shifting about so that the coffins beneath him rocked and creaked. He would not, he found, have to pile another on his platform to make the proper height, for the hole was on exactly the right level to use as soon as its size might permit.

It must have been midnight, at least, when Birch decided he could get through the transom. Tired and perspiring despite many rests, he descended to the floor and sat a while on the bottom box to gather strength for the final wriggle and leap to the ground outside.

The hungry horse was neighing repeatedly and almost uncannily, and he vaguely wished it would stop. He was curiously unelated over his impending escape and almost dreaded the exertion, for his form had the indolent stoutness of early middle age.

As he remounted the splitting coffins, he felt his weight very poignantly, especially when, upon reaching the topmost one, he heard that aggravated crackle that bespeaks the wholesale rending of wood.

He had, it seems, planned in vain when choosing the stoutest coffin for the platform, for no sooner was his full bulk again upon it than the rotting lid gave way, jouncing him two feet down on a surface that even he did not care to imagine.

Maddened by the sound or by the stench that billowed forth even into the open air, the waiting horse gave a scream that was too frantic for a neigh and plunged madly off through the night, the wagon rattling crazily behind it.

Birch, in his ghastly situation, was now too low for an easy scramble out of the enlarged transom, but he gathered his energies for a determined try.

Clutching the edges of the aperture, he sought to pull himself up, when he noticed a queer retardation in the form of an apparent drag on both his ankles.

In another moment, he knew fear for the first time that night, for struggle as he would, he could not shake clear of the unknown grasp that held his feet in relentless captivity.

Horrible pains, as of savage wounds, shot through his calves, and in his mind was a vortex of fright mixed with unquenchable materialism that suggested splinters, loose nails, or some other attribute of a breaking wooden box.

Perhaps he screamed. At any rate, he kicked and squirmed frantically and automatically while his consciousness was almost eclipsed in a half-swoon.

Instinct guided him in his wriggle through the transom and in the crawl that followed his jarring thud on the damp ground.

He could not walk, it appeared, and the emerging moon must have witnessed a horrible sight as he dragged his bleeding ankles toward the cemetery lodge, his fingers clawing the black mold in brainless haste, and his body responding with that maddening slowness from which one suffers when chased by the phantoms of a nightmare.

There was, however, no pursuer, for he was alone and alive when Armington, the lodgekeeper, answered his feeble clawing at the door.

Armington helped Birch to the outside of a spare bed and sent his little son Edwin for Dr. Davis. The afflicted man was fully conscious, but would say nothing of any consequence, merely muttering such things as 'Oh, my ankles!', 'let go!', or 'Shut in the tomb'.

Then the doctor came with his medicine case, asked crisp questions, and removed the patient's outer clothing, shoes, and socks.

The wounds – for both ankles were frightfully lacerated about the Achilles' tendons – seemed to puzzle the old physician greatly and finally almost frightened him.

His questioning grew more than medically tense, and his hands shook as he dressed the mangled members, binding them as if he wished to get the wounds out of sight as quickly as possible.

For an impersonal doctor, Davis' ominous and awestruck cross-examination became very strange indeed as he sought to drain from the weakened undertaker every last detail of his horrible experience. He was oddly anxious to know if Birch was sure – absolutely sure – of the identity of that top coffin of the pile, how he had chosen it, how he had been certain of it as the Fenner coffin in the dusk, and how he had distinguished it from the inferior duplicate coffin of vicious Asaph Sawyer.

Would the firm Fenner casket have caved in so readily? Davis, an old-time village practitioner, had of course seen both at the respective funerals, as indeed he had attended both Fenner and Sawyer in their last illnesses.

He had even wondered, at Sawyer's funeral, how the vindictive farmer had managed to lie straight in a box so closely akin to that of the diminutive Fenner.

After a full two hours, Dr. Davis left, urging Birch to insist at all times that his wounds were caused entirely by loose nails and splintering wood. What else, he added, could ever, in any case, be proved or believed?

But it would be well to say as little as could be said and to let no other doctor treat the wounds. Birch heeded this advice all the rest of his life till he told me his story, and when I saw the scars – ancient and whitened as they then were – I agreed that he was wise in so doing.

He always remained lame, for the great tendons had been severed, but I think the greatest lameness was in his soul. His thinking processes, once so phlegmatic and logical, had become ineffaceably scarred, and it was pitiful to note his response to certain chance allusions such as 'Friday', 'tomb', 'coffin', and words of less obvious concatenation.

His frightened horse had gone home, but his frightened wits never quite did that. He changed his business, but something always preyed on him. It may have been just fear, and it may have been fear mixed with a queer, belated sort of remorse for bygone crudities. His drinking, of course, only aggravated what it was meant to alleviate.

When Dr. Davis left Birch that night, he had taken a lantern and gone to the old receiving tomb. The moon was shining on the scattered brick fragments and marred facade, and the latch of the great door yielded readily to a touch from the outside. Steeled by old ordeals in dissecting rooms, the doctor entered and looked around, stifling the nausea of mind and body that everything in sight and smell induced.

He cried aloud once, and a little later, gave a gasp that was more terrible than a cry. Then he fled back to the lodge and broke all the rules of his calling by rousing and shaking his patient, and hurling at him a succession of shuddering whispers that seared into the bewildered ears like the hissing of vitriol.

»It was Asaph's coffin, Birch, just as I thought! I knew his teeth, with the front ones missing on the upper jaw – never, for God's sake, show those wounds! The body was pretty badly gone, but if ever I saw vindictiveness on any face – or former face ... «

»You know what a fiend he was for revenge – how he ruined old Raymond thirty years after their boundary suit, and how he stepped on the puppy that snapped at him a year ago last August ... «

»He was the devil incarnate, Birch, and I believe his eye-for-an-eye fury could beat old Father Death himself. God, what a rage! I'd hate to have it aimed at me!«

»Why did you do it, Birch? He was a scoundrel, and I don't blame you for giving him a cast-aside coffin, but you always did go too damn far! Well enough to skimp on the thing some way, but you knew what a little man old Fenner was.«

»I'll never get the picture out of my head as long as I live. You kicked hard, for Asaph's coffin was on the floor. His head was broken in, and everything was tumbled about. I've seen sights before, but there was one thing too much here. An eye for an eye! Great heavens, Birch, but you got what you deserved. The skull turned my stomach, but the other was worse – those ankles cut neatly off to fit Matt Fenner's cast-aside coffin!«

RATTLE OF BONES
by R.E. Howard (1929)

»Landlord, ho!« The shout broke the lowering silence and reverberated through the black forest with sinister echoing.

»This place hath a forbidding aspect, me seemeth.«

Two men stood in front of the forest tavern. The building was low, long, and rambling, built of heavy logs. Its small windows were heavily barred, and the door was closed. Above the door, its sinister sign showed faintly – a cleft skull.

This door swung slowly open, and a bearded face peered out. The owner of the face stepped back and motioned for his guests to enter – with a grudging gesture, it seemed. A candle gleamed on a table, and a flame smoldered in the fireplace.

»Your names?«

»Solomon Kane«, said the taller man briefly.

»Gaston l'Armon«, the other spoke curtly. »But what is that to you?«

»Strangers are few in the Black Forest«, grunted the host, »bandits many. Sit at yonder table, and I will bring food.«

The two men sat down with the bearing of men who had traveled far. One was a tall, gaunt man, clad in a featherless hat and somber black garments, which set off the dark pallor of his forbidding face. The other was of a different type entirely, bedecked with lace and plumes, although his finery was somewhat stained from travel. He was handsome in a bold way, and his restless eyes shifted from side to side, never still an instant.

The host brought wine and food to the rough-hewn table and then stood back in the shadows, like a somber image. His features, now receding into vagueness, now luridly etched in the firelight as it leaped and flickered, were masked in a beard that seemed almost animal-like in thickness. A great nose curved above this beard, and two small red eyes stared unblinkingly at his guests.

»Who are you?«, suddenly asked the younger man.

»I am the host of the Cleft Skull Tavern«, sullenly replied the other. His tone seemed to challenge his questioner to ask further.

»Do you have many guests?«, l'Armon pursued.

»Few come twice«, the host grunted.

Kane started and glanced up straight into those small red eyes as if he sought some hidden meaning in the host's words. The flaming eyes seemed to dilate, then dropped sullenly before the Englishman's cold stare.

»I'm for bed«, said Kane abruptly, bringing his meal to a close. »I must take up my journey by daylight.«

»And I«, added the Frenchman. »Host, show us to our chambers.«

Black shadows wavered on the walls as the two followed their silent host down a long, dark hall. The stocky, broad body of their guide seemed to grow and expand in the light of the small candle that he carried, throwing a long, grim shadow behind him.

At a certain door, he halted, indicating that they were to sleep there. They entered; the host lit a candle with the one he carried, then lurched back the way he had come.

In the chamber, the two men glanced at each other. The only furnishings in the room were a couple of bunk beds, a chair or two, and a heavy table.

»Let us see if there is any way to make fast the door«, said Kane. »I like not the looks of mine host.«

»There are racks on the door and jamb for a bar«, said Gaston, »but no bar.«

»We might break up the table and use its pieces for a bar,« mused Kane.

»Mon Dieu,« said l'Armon, »you are timorous, m'sieu.«

Kane scowled. »I like not being murdered in my sleep,« he answered gruffly.

»My faith!«, the Frenchman laughed. »We met by chance – until I overtook you on the forest road an hour before sunset, we had never seen each other.«

»I have seen you somewhere before«, answered Kane, »though I cannot now recall where. As for the other, I assume every man is an honest fellow until he shows me he is a rogue. Moreover, I am a light sleeper and slumber with a pistol at hand.«

The Frenchman laughed again.

»I was wondering how m'sieu could bring himself to sleep in the room with a stranger! Ha! Ha! All right, m'sieu Englishman, let us go forth and take a bar from one of the other rooms.«

Taking the candle with them, they went into the corridor. Utter silence reigned, and the small candle twinkled redly and evilly in the thick darkness.

»Mine host hath neither guests nor servants«, muttered Solomon Kane. »A strange tavern! What is the name, now? These German words come not easily to me – the Cleft Skull? A bloody name, I'faith.«

They tried the rooms next to theirs, but no bar rewarded their search. At last, they came to the last room at the end of the corridor. They entered. It was furnished like the rest, except that the door was provided with a small barred opening, and fastened from the outside with a heavy bolt, which was secured at one end to the door-jamb. They raised the bolt and looked in.

»There should be an outer window, but there is not«, muttered Kane. »Look!«

The floor was stained darkly. The walls and the one bunk were hacked in places, great splinters having been torn away.

»Men have died in here«, said Kane, somberly. »Is there not a bar fixed in the wall?«

»Aye, but 'tis made fast«, said the Frenchman, tugging at it. »The – «

A section of the wall swung back, and Gaston gave a quick exclamation. A small, secret room was revealed, and the two men bent over the grisly thing that lay on its floor.

»The skeleton of a man!«, said Gaston. »And behold, how his bony leg is shackled to the floor! He was imprisoned here and died.«

»Nay«, said Kane, »the skull is cleft – me thinks mine host had a grim reason for the name of his hellish tavern. This man, like us, was no doubt a wanderer who fell into the fiend's hands.«

»Likely«, said Gaston without interest. He was engaged in idly working the great iron ring from the skeleton's leg bones. Failing in this, he drew his sword and, with an exhibition of remarkable strength, cut the chain that joined the ring on the leg to a ring set deep in the log floor.

»Why should he shackle a skeleton to the floor?«, mused the Frenchman. »Monbleu! 'Tis a waste of good chain. Now, m'sieu«, he ironically addressed the white heap of bones, »I have freed you, and you may go where you like!«

»Have done!« Kane's voice was deep. »No good will come of mocking the dead.«

»The dead should defend themselves«, laughed l'Armon. »Somehow, I will slay the man who kills me, though my corpse climbs up forty fathoms of the ocean to do it.«

Kane turned toward the outer door, closing the door of the secret room behind him. He did not like this talk, which smacked of demonry and witchcraft, and he was in haste to face the host with the charge of his guilt.

As he turned, with his back to the Frenchman, he felt the touch of cold steel against his neck and knew that a pistol muzzle was pressed close beneath the base of his brain.

»Move not, m'sieu!« The voice was low and silky. »Move not, or I will scatter your few brains over the room.«

The Puritan, raging inwardly, stood with his hands in the air while l'Armon slipped his pistols and sword from their sheaths.

»Now you can turn«, said Gaston, stepping back.

Kane bent a grim eye on the dapper fellow, who stood bareheaded now, hat in one hand, the other hand leveling his long pistol.

»Gaston the Butcher!«, said the Englishman somberly. »Fool that I was to trust a Frenchman! You range far, murderer! I remember you now, with that cursed great hat off – I saw you in Calais some years ago.«

»Aye – and now you will see me never again. What was that?«

»Rats exploring yon skeleton«, said Kane, watching the bandit like a hawk, waiting for a single slight wavering of that black gun muzzle. »The sound was of the rattle of bones.«

»Like enough«, returned the other. »Now, M'sieu Kane, I know you carry considerable money on your person. I had thought to wait until you slept and then slay you, but the opportunity presented itself, and I took it. You trick easily.«

»I had little thought that I should fear a man with whom I had broken bread«, said Kane, a deep timbre of slow fury sounding in his voice.

The bandit laughed cynically. His eyes narrowed as he began to back slowly toward the outer door. Kane's sinews tensed involuntarily; he gathered himself like a giant wolf about to launch himself in a death leap, but Gaston's hand was like a rock, and the pistol never trembled.

»We will have no death plunges after the shot«, said Gaston. »Stand still, m'sieu. I have seen men killed by dying men, and I wish to have enough distance between us to preclude that possibility. My faith – I will shoot, you will roar and charge, but you will die before you reach me with your bare hands. And mine host will have another skeleton in his secret niche. That is if I do not kill him myself. The fool knows me not, nor I him, moreover – «

The Frenchman was in the doorway now, sighting along the barrel. The candle, which had been stuck in a niche on the wall, shed a weird and flickering light that did not extend past the doorway. And with the suddenness of death, from the darkness behind Gaston's back, a broad, vague form rose up, and a gleaming blade swept down. The Frenchman went to his knees like a butchered ox, his brains spilling from his cleft skull. Above him towered the figure of the host, a wild and terrible spectacle, still holding the hanger with which he had slain the bandit.

»Ho! ho!«, he roared. »Back!«

Kane had leaped forward as Gaston fell, but the host thrust into his very face a long pistol, which he held in his left hand.

»Back!«, he repeated in a tigerish roar, and Kane retreated from the menacing weapon and the insanity in the red eyes.

The Englishman stood silent, his flesh crawling as he sensed a deeper and more hideous threat than the Frenchman had offered. There was something inhuman about this man, who now swayed to and fro like some great forest beast while his mirthless laughter boomed out again.

»Gaston the Butcher!«, he shouted, kicking the corpse at his feet. »Ho! ho! My fine brigand will hunt no more! I had heard of this fool who roamed the Black Forest – he wished gold, and he found death! Now your gold shall be mine, and more than gold – vengeance!«

»I am no foe of yours«, Kane spoke calmly.

»All men are my foes! Look – the marks on my wrists! See – the marks on my ankles! And deep in my back – the kiss of the knout! And deep in my brain, the wounds of the years of the cold, silent cells where I lay as punishment for a crime I never committed!«

The voice broke into a hideous, grotesque sob.

Kane made no answer. This man was not the first he had seen whose brain had shattered amid the horrors of the terrible Continental prisons.

»But I escaped!«, the scream rose triumphantly. »And here I make war on all men ... What was that?«

Did Kane see a flash of fear in those hideous eyes?

»My sorcerer is rattling his bones!«, whispered the host, then laughed wildly. »Dying, he swore his very bones would weave a net of death for me. I shackled his corpse to the floor, and now, deep in the night, I hear his bare skeleton clash and rattle as he seeks to be free, and I laugh, I laugh! Ho! ho! How he yearns to rise and stalk like old King Death along these dark corridors when I sleep, to slay me in my bed!«

Suddenly the insane eyes flared hideously: »You were in that secret room, you and this dead fool! Did he talk to you?«

Kane shuddered, completely beside himself. Was it insanity, or did he actually hear the faint rattle of bones, as if the skeleton had moved slightly? Kane shrugged his shoulders. Rats will even tug at dusty bones.

The host was laughing again. He sidled around Kane, keeping the Englishman always covered, and with his free hand, he opened the door. All was darkness within, so Kane could not even see the glimmer of the bones on the floor.

»All men are my foes!«, mumbled the host, in the incoherent manner of the insane. »Why should I spare any man? Who lifted a hand to my aid when I lay for years in the vile dungeons of Karlsruhe – and for a deed never proven? Something happened to my brain, then. I became like a wolf – a brother to these of the Black Forest to which I fled when I escaped.«

»They have feasted, my brothers, on all who lay in my tavern – all except this one who now clashes his bones, this magician from Russia. Lest he come stalking back through the black shadows, when the night is over the world, and slay me – for who may slay the dead? – I stripped his bones and shackled him. His sorcery was not powerful enough to save him from me, but all men know that a dead magician is more evil than a living one. Move not, Englishman! Your bones I shall leave in this secret room beside this one, to – «

The maniac was now standing partly in the doorway of the secret room, his weapon still menacing Kane. Suddenly he seemed to topple backward and vanish in the darkness, and at the same instant, a vagrant gust of wind swept down the outer corridor and slammed the door shut behind him. The candle on the wall flickered and went out. Kane's groping hands, sweeping over the floor, found a pistol, and he straightened, facing the door where the maniac had vanished. He stood in the utter darkness, his blood freezing, while a hideous muffled screaming came from the secret room, intermingled with the dry, grisly rattle of fleshless bones. Then silence fell.

Kane found flint and steel and lit the candle. Then, holding it in one hand and the pistol in the other, he opened the secret door.

»Great God!«, he muttered as cold sweat formed on his body. »This thing is beyond all reason, yet with mine own eyes I see it! Two vows have been kept here, for Gaston the Butcher swore that even in death he would avenge his slaying, and his was the hand that set yon fleshless monster free. And he – «

The host of the Cleft Skull lay lifeless on the floor of the secret room, his bestial face set in lines of terrible fear, and deep in his broken neck were sunk the bare fingerbones of the sorcerer's skeleton.

THE MONKEY'S PAW
by W.W. Jacobs (1902)

I.

Without, the night was cold and wet, but in the small parlor of Laburnum Villa, the blinds were drawn and the fire burned brightly. Father and son were at chess; the former, who possessed ideas about the game involving radical chances, putting his king into such sharp and unnecessary perils that it even provoked a comment from the white-haired old lady knitting placidly by the fire.

»Hark at the wind«, said Mr. White, who, having seen a fatal mistake after it was too late, was amiably desirous of preventing his son from seeing it.

»I'm listening«, said the latter, grimly surveying the board as he stretched out his hand. »Check.«

»I should hardly think that he's come tonight«, said his father, with his hand poised over the board.

»Mate«, replied the son.

»That's the worst of living so far out«, balled Mr. White with sudden and unlooked-for violence. »Of all the beastly, slushy, out-of-the-way places to live, this is the worst. The path's a bog, and the road's a torrent. I don't know what people are thinking about. I suppose because only two houses in the road are left, they think it doesn't matter.«

»Never mind, dear«, said his wife soothingly; »perhaps you'll win the next one.«

Mr. White looked up sharply, just in time to intercept a knowing glance between mother and son. The words died away on his lips, and he hid a guilty grin in his thin gray beard.

»There he is«, said Herbert White as the gate banged too loudly and heavy footsteps came toward the door.

The old man rose with hospitable haste and, opening the door, was heard lamenting about the roads. The new arrival also lamented, so that Mrs. White said, »Tut, tut!«, and coughed gently as her husband entered the room, followed by a tall, burly man, beady of eye and rubicund of visage.

»Sergeant-Major Morris«, he said, introducing him.

The Sergeant-Major took hands and, taking the proffered seat by the fire, watched contentedly as his host got out whiskey and tumblers and stood a small copper kettle on the fire.

At the third glass, his eyes got brighter, and he began to talk, the little family circle regarding with eager interest this visitor from distant parts, as he squared his broad shoulders in the chair and spoke of wild scenes and doughty deeds, of wars and plagues and strange peoples.

»Twenty-one years of it«, said Mr. White, nodding at his wife and son. »When he went away, he was a slip of a youth in the warehouse. Now look at him.«

»He doesn't look to have taken much harm«, said Mrs. White politely.

»I'd like to go to India myself«, said the old man, just to look around a bit, you know.«

»Better where you are«, said the Sergeant-Major, shaking his head. He put down the empty glass and, sighing softly, shook it again.

»I should like to see those old temples and fakirs and jugglers«, said the old man. »What was that that you started telling me the other day about a monkey's paw or something, Morris?«

»Nothing«, said the soldier hastily. »Leastways, nothing worth hearing.«

»Monkey's paw?«, said Mrs. White curiously.

»Well, it's just a bit of what you might call magic, perhaps«, said the Sergeant-Major off-handedly.

His three listeners leaned forward eagerly. The visitor absent-mindedly put his empty glass to his lips and then set it down again. His host filled it for him again.

»To look at«, said the Sergeant-Major, fumbling in his pocket, »it's just an ordinary little paw, dried to a mummy.«

He took something out of his pocket and proffered it. Mrs. White drew back with a grimace, but her son, taking it, examined it curiously.

»And what is there special about it?«, inquired Mr. White as he took it from his son, and having examined it, he placed it upon the table.

»It had a spell put on it by an old Fakir«, said the Sergeant-Major, »a very holy man. He wanted to show that fate ruled people's lives, and that those who interfered with it did so to their sorrow. He put a spell on it so that three separate men could each have three wishes from it.«

His manners were so impressive that his hearers were conscious that their light laughter had jarred somewhat.

»Well, why don't you have three, sir?«, said Herbert White cleverly.

The soldier regarded him the way that middle age is wont to regard presumptuous youth. »I have«, he said quietly, and his blotchy face whitened.

»And did you really have the three wishes granted?«, asked Mrs. White.

»I did«, said the sergeant-major, and his glass tapped against his strong teeth.

»And has anybody else wished?«, persisted the old lady.

»The first man had his three wishes. Yes,« was the reply. »I don't know what the first two were, but the third was for death. That's how I got the paw.«

His tones were so grave that a hush fell upon the group.

»If you've had your three wishes, it's no good to you anymore, Morris«, said the old man at last. »What do you keep it for?«

The soldier shook his head. »Fancy, I suppose«, he said slowly. »I did have some idea of selling it, but I don't think I will. It has caused me enough mischief already. Besides, people won't buy it. Some of them think it's a fairy tale; and those who do think anything of it want to try it first and pay me afterward.«

»If you could have another three wishes«, said the old man, eyeing him keenly«, would you have them?«

»I don't know«, said the other. »I don't know.«

He took the paw and, dangling it between his forefinger and thumb, suddenly threw it into the fire. White, with a slight cry, stooped down and snatched it off.

»Better let it burn«, said the soldier solemnly.

»If you don't want it, Morris«, said the other, »give it to me.«

»I won't«, said his friend doggedly. »I threw it on the fire. If you keep it, don't blame me for what happens. Pitch it on the fire like a sensible man.«

The other shook his head and examined his possession closely. »How do you do it?«, he inquired.

»Hold it up in your right hand and wish aloud«, said the Sergeant-Major, »but I warn you of the consequences.«

»Sounds like the 'Arabian Nights'«, said Mrs. White, as she rose and began to set the supper. »Don't you think you might wish for four pairs of hands for me?«

Her husband drew the talisman from his pocket, and all three burst into laughter as the Seargent-Major, with a look of alarm on his face, caught him by the arm.

»If you must wish«, he said gruffly, »wish for something sensible.«

Mr. White dropped it back in his pocket and, placing chairs, motioned his friend to the table. In the business of supper, the talisman was partly forgotten, and afterward, the three sat listening in an enthralled fashion to a second installment of the soldier's adventures in India.

»If the tale about the monkey's paw is not more truthful than those he has been telling us«, said Herbert, as the door closed behind their guest, just in time to catch the last train, »we shan't make much out of it.«

»Did you give anything for it, father?«, inquired Mrs. White, regarding her husband closely.

»A trifle«, said he, coloring slightly. »He didn't want it, but I made him take it. And he pressed me again to throw it away.«

»Likely«, said Herbert, with pretended horror. »Why, we're going to be rich and famous and happy. Wish to be an emperor, father, to begin with; then you can't be henpecked.«

He darted around the table, pursued by the maligned Mrs. White, armed with an antimacassar.

Mr. White took the paw from his pocket and eyed it dubiously. »I don't know what to wish for, and that's a fact«, he said slowly. It seems to me I've got all I want.«

»If you only cleared the house, you'd be quite happy, wouldn't you!« said Herbert, with his hand on his shoulder. »Well, wish for two hundred pounds, then; that'll just do it.«

His father, smiling shamefacedly at his own credulity, held up the talisman, as his son, with a solemn face, somewhat marred by a wink at his mother, sat down and struck a few impressive chords.

»I wish for *two hundred pounds*«, said the old man distinctly.

A fine crash from the piano greeted his words, interrupted by a shuddering cry from the old man. His wife and son ran toward him.

»It moved«, he cried, with a glance of disgust at the object as it lay on the floor. »As I wished, it twisted in my hand like a snake.«

»Well, I don't see the money«, said his son, as he picked it up and placed it on the table, »and I bet I never shall.«

»It must have been your fancy, father«, said his wife, regarding him anxiously.

He shook his head. »Never mind, though; there's no harm done, but it gave me a shock all the same.«

They sat down by the fire again while the two men finished their pipes. Outside, the wind was higher than ever, and the old man started nervously at the sound of a door banging upstairs. A strange and depressing silence settled on all three, which lasted until the old couple rose to retire for the rest of the night.

»I expect you'll find the cash tied up in a big bag in the middle of your bed«, said Herbert, as he bade them good night, »and something horrible squatting on top of your wardrobe watching you as you pocket your ill-gotten gains.«

He sat alone in the darkness, gazing at the dying fire, and seeing faces in it. The last was so horrible and so simian that he gazed at it in amazement. It got so vivid that, with a little uneasy laugh, he felt on the table for a glass containing a little water to throw over it. His hand grasped the monkey's paw, and with a little shiver, he wiped his hand on his coat and went up to bed.

II.

In the brightness of the wintry sun next morning, as it streamed over the breakfast table, he laughed at his fears. There was an air of prosaic wholesomeness about the room that it had lacked the previous night, and the dirty, shriveled little paw was pitched on the sideboard with a carelessness that betokened no great belief in its virtues.

»I suppose all old soldiers are the same«, said Mrs. White. »The idea of our listening to such nonsense! How could wishes be granted these days? And if they could, how could two hundred pounds hurt you, father?«

»Might drop on his head from the sky«, said the frivolous Herbert.

»Morris said the things happened so naturally«, said his father, »that you might, if you so wished, attribute it to coincidence.«

»Well, don't break into the money before I come back«, said Herbert as he rose from the table. »I'm afraid it'll turn you into a mean, avaricious man, and we shall have to disown you.«

His mother laughed, and following him to the door, she watched him down the road. Returning to the breakfast table, she was very happy at the expense of her husband's credulity. All of which did not prevent her from scurrying to the door at the postman's knock, nor did it prevent her from referring somewhat shortly to retired Sergeant-Majors of bibulous habits when she found that the post brought a tailor's bill.

»Herbert will have some more of his funny remarks, I expect, when he comes home«, she said as they sat at dinner.

»I dare say«, said Mr. White, pouring himself out some beer; »but for all that, the thing moved in my hand, and that I'll swear to.«

»You thought it did«, said the old lady soothingly.

»I say it did«, replied the other. »There was no thought about it; I had just – what's the matter?«

His wife made no reply. She was watching the mysterious movements of a man outside, who, peering in an undecided fashion at the house, appeared to be trying to make up his mind to enter.

In mental connection with the two hundred pounds, she noticed that the stranger was well dressed and wore a silk hat of glossy newness. Three times, he paused at the gate and then walked on again. The fourth time, he stood with his hand upon it, and then, with sudden resolution, flung it open and walked up the path.

Mrs. White, at the same moment, placed her hands behind her and, hurriedly unfastening the strings of her apron, put that useful article of apparel beneath the cushion of her chair.

She brought the stranger, who seemed ill at ease, into the room. He gazed at her furtively and listened in a preoccupied fashion as the old lady apologized for the appearance of the room, and her husband's coat, a garment that he usually reserved for the garden. She then waited as patiently as her sex would permit for him to broach his business, but he was at first strangely silent.

»I – was asked to call«, he said at last, and stooped and took out a piece of cotton from his trousers. »I come from 'Maw and Meggins'.«

The old lady started. »Is anything the matter?«, she asked breathlessly. »Has anything happened to Herbert? What is it? What is it?«

Her husband interposed. »There, there, mother«, he said hastily. »Sit down, and don't jump to conclusions. You've not brought bad news, I'm sure, sir,« and eyed the other wistfully.

»I'm sorry – «, began the visitor.

»Is he hurt?«, demanded the mother wildly.

The visitor bowed in assent. »Badly hurt«, he said quietly, »but he is not in any pain.«

»Oh, thank God!«, said the old woman, clasping her hands. »Thank God for that! Thank – «

She broke off as the sinister meaning of the assurance dawned on her, and she saw the awful confirmation of her fears in the other's averted face.

She caught her breath and, turning to her slower-witted husband, laid her trembling hand on his. There was a long silence.

»He was caught in the machinery«, said the visitor at length in a low voice.

»Caught in the machinery«, repeated Mr. White in a dazed fashion, »yes.«

He sat staring out the window and, taking his wife's hand between his own, pressed it as he had been wont to do in their old courting days nearly forty years before.

»He was the only one left to us«, he said, turning gently to the visitor. »It is hard.«

The other coughed, rose, and walked slowly to the window. »The firm wishes me to convey their sincere sympathy with you in your great loss«, he said without looking around. »I beg that you will understand, I am only their servant, merely obeying orders.«

There was no reply; the old woman's face was white, her eyes staring, and her breath inaudible; on the husband's face was a look such as his friend the sergeant might have carried into his first action.

»I was to say that Maw and Meggins disclaim all responsibility«, continued the other. »They admit no liability at all, but in consideration of your son's services, they wish to present you with a certain sum as compensation.«

Mr. White dropped his wife's hand and, rising to his feet, gazed with a look of horror at his visitor. His dry lips shaped the words: »How much?«

»*Two hundred pounds*«, was the answer.

Unconscious of his wife's shriek, the old man smiled faintly, put out his hands like a sightless man, and dropped a senseless heap to the floor.

III.

In the huge new cemetery, some two miles away, the old people buried their dead and came back to the house steeped in shadows and silence. It was all over so quickly that at first they could hardly realize it and remained in a state of expectation, as though of something else to happen - something else that was to lighten this load, too heavy for old hearts to bear.

But the days passed, and expectations gave way to resignation - the hopeless resignation of the old, sometimes miscalled apathy. Sometimes they hardly exchanged a word, as for now, they had nothing to talk about, and their days were long to wear.

It was about a week after, that the old man, awaking suddenly in the night, stretched out his hand and found himself alone. The room was in darkness, and the sound of subdued weeping came from the window. He raised himself in bed and listened.

»Come back«, he said tenderly. »You will be cold.«

»It is colder for my son«, said the old woman, and wept afresh.

The sounds of her sobs died away in his ears. The bed was warm, and his eyes were heavy with sleep. He dozed fitfully and then slept until a sudden wild cry from his wife awoke him with a start.

»THE PAW!«, she cried wildly, »THE MONKEY'S PAW!«

He started up in alarm. »Where? Where is it? What's the matter?«

She came stumbling across the room toward him. »I want it,« she said quietly. »You've not destroyed it?«

»It's in the parlor, on the bracket«, he replied, marveling. »Why?«

She cried and laughed together, and bending over, kissed his cheek.

»I only just thought of it«, she said hysterically. »Why didn't I think of it before? Why didn't you think of it?«

»Think of what?«, he questioned.

»The other two wishes«, she replied rapidly. »We've only had one.«

»Was not that enough?«, he demanded fiercely.

»No«, she cried triumphantly. »We'll have one more. Go down and get it quickly, and wish our boy alive again.«

The man sat in bed and flung the bedclothes from his quaking limbs. »Good God, you are mad!«, he cried aghast.

»Get it«, she panted; »get it quickly, and wish – oh my boy, my boy!«

Her husband struck a match and lit the candle. »Get back to bed, he said unsteadily. »You don't know what you are saying.«

»We had the first wish granted«, said the old woman, feverishly, »why not the second?«

»A coincidence«, stammered the old man.

»Go get it and wish«, cried his wife, quivering with excitement.

The old man turned and regarded her, and his voice shook.

»He has been dead for ten days, and besides he – I would not tell you else, but – I could only recognize him by his clothing. If he was too terrible for you to see then, how now?«

»Bring him back«, cried the old woman, and dragged him towards the door. »Do you think I fear the child I have nursed?«

He went down in the darkness, and felt his way to the parlor, and then to the mantlepiece. The talisman was in its place, and a horrible fear that the unspoken wish might bring his mutilated son before him ere he could escape from the room seized up on him, and he caught his breath as he found that he had lost the direction of the door. His brow cold with sweat, he felt his way around the table and groped along the wall until he found himself in the small passage with the unwholesome thing in his hand.

Even his wife's face seemed changed as he entered the room. It was white and expectant and, to his fears, seemed to have an unnatural look upon it. He was afraid of her.

»WISH!«, she cried in a strong voice.

»It is foolish and wicked«, he faltered.

»WISH!«, repeated his wife.

He raised his hand. »I wish my son alive again.«

The talisman fell to the floor, and he regarded it fearfully. Then he sank trembling into a chair as the old woman, with burning eyes, walked to the window and raised the blind.

He sat until he was chilled with the cold, glancing occasionally at the figure of the old woman peering through the window. The candle-end, which had burned below the rim of the China candlestick, was throwing pulsating shadows on the ceiling and walls, until, with a flicker larger than the rest, it expired. The old man, with an unspeakable sense of relief at the failure of the talisman, crept back to his bed, and a minute afterward, the old woman came silently and apathetically beside him.

Neither spoke. They were wordlessly listening to the ticking of the clock. A stair creaked, and a squeaky mouse scurried noisily through the wall. The darkness was oppressive, and after lying for some time, screwing up his courage, he took the box of matches and, striking one, went downstairs for a candle.

At the foot of the stairs, the match went out, and he paused to strike another; and at the same moment, a knock that came so quiet and stealthy as to be scarcely audible, sounded on the front door.

The matches fell from his hand and spilled in the passage. He stood motionless, his breath suspended, until the knock was repeated. Then he turned and fled swiftly back to his room, and closed the door behind him. A third knock sounded through the house.

»WHAT'S THAT?«, cried the old woman, starting up.

»A rat«, said the old man in shaking tones – »a rat. It passed me on the stairs.«

His wife sat up in bed, listening. A loud knock resounded through the house.

»It's Herbert!«

She ran to the door, but her husband was before her, and catching her by the arm, held her tightly.

»What are you going to do?«, he whispered hoarsely.

»It's my boy; it's Herbert!«, she cried, struggling mechanically. »I forgot it was two miles away. What are you holding me for? Let go. I must open the door.«

»For God's sake, don't let it in«, cried the old man, trembling.

»You're afraid of your own son«, she cried, struggling. »Let me go. I'm coming, Herbert, I'm coming.«

There was another knock, and another. The old woman, with a sudden wrench, broke free and ran from the room. Her husband followed her to the landing and called after her appealingly as she hurried downstairs. He heard the chain rattle back, and the bolt was drawn slowly and stiffly from the socket. Then the old woman's voice strained and panted.

»The bolt«, she cried loudly. »Come down. I can't reach it.«

But her husband was on his hands and knees, groping wildly on the floor in search of the paw. If only he could find it before the thing outside got in.

A perfect fusillade of knocks reverberated through the house, and he heard the scraping of a chair as his wife put it down in the passage against the door.

He heard the creaking of the bolt as it came slowly back, and at the same moment, he found the monkey's paw, and frantically breathed his third and last wish.

The knocking ceased suddenly, although the echoes of it were still in the house. He heard the chair drawn back, and the door opened.

A cold wind rushed up the staircase, and a long, loud wail of disappointment and misery from his wife gave him the courage to run down to her side, and then to the gate beyond.

The street lamp flickering opposite shone on a quiet and deserted road.

THE GHOST-EXTINGUISHER
by Gelett Burgess (1905)

My attention was first called to the possibility of manufacturing a practicable ghost-extinguisher by a real estate agent in San Francisco.

»There's one thing«, he said, »that affects city property here in a curious way. You know we have a good many murders, and, as a consequence, certain houses attain a very sensational and undesirable reputation. These houses are almost impossible to let; you can scarcely get a decent family to occupy them rent-free. Then we have a great many places said to be haunted. These were dead timber on my hands until I happened to notice that the Japanese have no objections to spooks. Now, whenever I have such a building to rent, I let it to Japs at a nominal figure, and after they've taken the curse off, I raise the rent, the Japs move out, the place is renovated, and it is in the market again.«

The subject interested me, for I am not only a scientist, but a speculative philosopher as well. The investigation of those phenomena that lie upon the threshold of the great unknown has always been my favorite field of research.

I believed, even then, that the Oriental mind, working along different lines than those which we pursue, has attained knowledge that we know little of.

Thinking, therefore, that these Japs might have some secret inherited from their misty past, I examined the matter.

I shall not trouble you with a narration of the incidents that led up to my acquaintance with Hoku Yamanochi. Suffice it to say that I found in him a friend who was willing to share with me his whole lore of quasi-science. I call it this advisedly, for science, as we Occidentals use the term, has to do only with the laws of matter and sensation; our scientific men, in fact, recognize the existence of nothing else. The Buddhistic philosophy, however, goes further.

According to its theories, the soul is sevenfold, consisting of different shells or envelopes – something like an onion – that are shed as life passes from the material to the spiritual state. The first, or lowest, of these is the corporeal body, which, after death, decays and perishes.

Next comes the vital principle, which, departing from the body, dissipates itself like an odor, and is lost. Less gross than this is the astral body, which, although immaterial, yet lies near to the consistency of matter. This astral shape, released from the body at death, remains for a while in its earthly environment, still preserving more or less definitely the imprint of the form which it inhabited.

It is this relic of a past material personality, this outworn shell, that appears, when galvanized into an appearance of life, partly materialized, as a ghost. It is not the soul that returns, for the soul, which is immortal, is composed of the four higher spiritual essences that surround the ego, and are carried on into the next life. These astral bodies, therefore, fail to terrify the Buddhists, who know them only as shadows, with no real volition. The Japs, as a matter of fact, have learned how to exterminate them.

There is a certain powder, Hoku informed me, that, when burned in their presence, transforms them from the rarefied, or semi-spiritual, condition to the state of matter. The ghost, so to speak, is precipitated into and becomes a material shape that can easily be disposed of. In this state, it is confined and allowed to disintegrate slowly, where it can cause no further annoyance.

This long-winded explanation piqued my curiosity, which was not satisfied until I had seen the Japanese method applied. It was not long before I had an opportunity. A particularly revolting murder having been committed in San Francisco, my friend Hoku Yamanochi applied for the house, and, after the police had finished their examination, he was permitted to occupy it for a half-year at the ridiculous price of three dollars a month. He invited me to share his quarters, which were large and luxuriously furnished.

For a week, nothing abnormal occurred.

Then, one night, I was awakened by terrifying groans followed by a blood-curdling shriek that seemed to emerge from a large closet in my room, the scene of the late atrocity.

I confess that I had all the covers pulled over my head and was shivering with horror when my Japanese friend entered, wearing a pair of flowered-silk pajamas. Hearing his voice, I peeped forward, to see him smiling reassuringly.

»You some kind of very foolish fellow«, he said. »I show you how to fix him!«

He took from his pocket three conical red pastilles, placed them on a saucer and lit them. Then, holding the fuming dish in one outstretched hand, he walked to the closed door and opened it. The shrieks burst out afresh, and, as I recalled the appalling details of the scene that had occurred in this very room only five weeks ago, I shuddered at his temerity. But he was quite calm.

Soon, I saw the wraith-like form of the recent victim dart from the closet. She crawled under my bed and ran about the room, endeavoring to escape, but was pursued by Hoku, who waved his smoking plate with indefatigable patience and dexterity.

At last, he had her cornered, and the specter was caught behind a curtain of odorous fumes. Slowly, the figure grew more distinct, assuming the consistency of a heavy vapor, shrinking somewhat in the operation. Hoku now hurriedly turned to me.

»You hully up, bling me one pair bellows pletty quick!«, he commanded.

I ran into his room and brought the bellows from his fireplace. These he pressed flat, and then carefully inserting one toe of the ghost into the nozzle and opening the handles steadily, he sucked in a portion of the unfortunate woman's anatomy, and dexterously squirted the vapor into a large jar, which had been placed in the room for the purpose.

Two more operations were necessary to withdraw the phantom completely from the corner and empty it into the jar. At last, the transfer was effected, and the receptacle was securely stoppered and sealed.

»In formel time«, Hoku explained to me, »old pliests sucked ghost with mouth and spit him to inside of vase with acculacy. Modern-time method more better for stomach and epiglottis.«

»How long will this ghost last?«, I inquired.

»Oh, about four, five hundled years, maybe«, was his reply. »Ghost now change from spilit to matter, and comes under legality of matter as usual science.«

»What are you going to do with her?« I asked.

»Send her to Buddhist temple in Japan. Old pliest use her for high celemony«, was the answer.

My next desire was to obtain some of Hoku Yamanochi's ghost-powder and analyze it.

For a while, it defied my attempts, but, after many months of patient research, I discovered that it could be produced, in all its essential qualities, by means of a fusion of formaldehyde and hypophenyltry-brompropionic acid in an electrified vacuum. With this product, I began a series of interesting experiments.

As it became necessary for me to discover the habitat of ghosts in considerable numbers, I joined the American Society for Psychical Research, thus securing desirable information in regard to haunted houses. These I visited persistently, until my powder was perfected and had been proven efficacious for the capture of any ordinary house-broken phantom.

For a while, I contented myself with the mere sterilization of these specters, but, as I became surer of success, I began to attempt the transfer of ghosts to receptacles wherein they could be transported and studied at my leisure, classified, and preserved for future reference.

Hoku's bellows I soon discarded in favor of a large-sized bicycle-pump, and eventually I had constructed one of my own, of a pattern that enabled me to inhale an entire ghost in a single stroke. With this powerful instrument, I was able to compress even an adult life-sized ghost into a two-quart bottle, in the neck of which a sensitive valve (patented) prevented the specter from emerging during the process.

My invention was not yet, however, quite satisfactory.

While I had no trouble securing ghosts of recent creation – spirits, that is, who were yet of almost the consistency of matter – on several of my trips abroad in search of material, I found in old manor houses or ruined castles many specters so ancient that they had become highly rarefied and tenuous, being at times scarcely visible to the naked eye. Such elusive spirits are able to pass through walls and elude pursuit with ease. It became necessary for me to obtain some instrument by which their capture could be conveniently effected.

The ordinary fire-extinguisher of commerce gave me the hint as to how the problem could be solved.

One of these portable hand-instruments I filled with the proper chemicals. When inverted, the ingredients were commingled in vacuo, and a vast volume of gas was liberated. This was collected in the reservoir, provided with a rubber tube with a nozzle at the end. With the whole apparatus being strapped to my back, I was able to direct a stream of powerful precipitating gas in any desired direction, with the flow being under control through the agency of a small stopcock. By means of this ghost-extinguisher, I was enabled to pursue my experiments as far as I desired.

So far, my investigations have been purely scientific, but before long, the commercial value of my discovery began to interest me. The ruinous effects of spectral visitations upon real estate induced me to realize some pecuniary reward from my ghost-extinguisher, and I began to advertise my business. By degrees, I became known as an expert in my original line, and my professional services were sought with as much confidence as those of a veterinary surgeon. I manufactured the Gerrish Ghost-Extinguisher in several sizes, and put it on the market, following this venture with the introduction of my justly celebrated Gerrish Ghost-Grenades. These hand-implements were made to be kept in racks conveniently distributed in country houses for cases of sudden emergencies. A single grenade, hurled at any spectral form, would, in breaking, liberate enough formaldybrom to coagulate the most perverse spirit, and the resulting vapor could easily be removed from the room by a housemaid with a common broom.

This branch of my business, however, never proved profitable, for the appearance of ghosts, especially in the United States, is seldom anticipated. Had it been possible for me to invent a preventive as well as a remedy, I might now be a millionaire, but there are limits even to modern science.

Having exhausted the field at home, I visited England in the hope of securing customers among the country families there. To my surprise, I discovered that the possession of a family specter was considered as a permanent improvement to the property, and my offers of service in ridding houses of ghostly tenants awakened the liveliest resentment. As a layer of ghosts, I was much lower on the social scale than a layer of carpets.

Disappointed and discouraged, I returned home to make further studies of the opportunities of my invention. I had, it seemed, exhausted the possibilities of the use of unwelcome phantoms. Could I not, I thought, derive a revenue from the traffic in desirable specters? I decided to renew my investigation.

The nebulous spirits preserved in my laboratory, which I had graded and classified, were, you will remember, in a state of suspended animation. They were, virtually, embalmed apparitions, their inevitable decay delayed, rather than prevented. The assorted ghosts that I had now preserved in hermetically sealed tins were thus in a state of unstable equilibrium. Once the tins were opened and the vapor allowed to dissipate, the original astral body would in time be reconstructed, and the warmed-over specter would continue its previous career. But this process, when naturally performed, took years. The interval was quite too long for the phantom to be handled in any commercial way. My problem was, therefore, to produce from my tinned 'Essence of Ghost' a specter that was capable of immediately going into business and that could haunt a house while you waited.

It was not until radium was discovered that I approached the solution to my great problem, and even then, months of indefatigable labor were necessary before the process was perfected. It has now been well demonstrated that the emanations of radiant energy sent forth by this surprising element defy our former scientific conceptions of the constitution of matter. It was for me to prove that the vibratory activity of radium (whose amplitudes and intensity are undoubtedly four-dimensional) effects a sort of allotropic modification in the particles of that imponderable ether, which seems to lie halfway between matter and pure spirit. This is as far as I need to go in my explanation, for a full discussion involves the use of quaternions and the method of least squares. It will be sufficient for the layman to know that my preserved phantoms, rendered radioactive, would, upon contact with the air, resume their spectral shape.

The possible extension of my business now was enormous, limited only by the difficulty in collecting the necessary stock. It was by this time almost as difficult to get ghosts as it was to get radium. Finding that a part of my stock had spoiled, I was now possessed of only a few dozen cans of apparitions, many of these were of inferior quality. I immediately set about replenishing my raw materials. It was not enough for me to pick up a ghost here and there, as one might get old mahogany; I determined to procure my phantoms in wholesale lots.

Accident favored my design. In an old volume of Blackwood's Magazine, I happened, one day, to come across an interesting article on the battle of Waterloo. It mentioned, incidentally, a legend to the effect that every year, upon the anniversary of the celebrated victory, spectral squadrons had been seen by the peasants charging battalions of ghostly grenadiers. Here was my opportunity.

I made elaborate preparations for the capture of this job lot of phantoms upon the next anniversary of the fight. Hard by the fatal ditch that engulfed Napoleon's cavalry, I stationed a corps of able assistants provided with rapid-fire extinguishers, ready to enfilade the famous sunken road. I stationed myself with a model No. 4 magazine hose with a four-inch nozzle, directly in the path that I knew would be taken by the advancing squadron.

It was a fine, clear night, lighted, at first, by a slice of new moon, but later, dark, except for the pale illumination of the stars. I have seen many ghosts in my time – ghosts in garden and garret, at noon, at dusk, at dawn, phantoms fanciful, and specters sad and spectacular – but never have I seen such an impressive sight as this nocturnal charge of cuirassiers, galloping in goblin glory to their time-honored doom. From afar, the French reserves presented the appearance of a nebulous mass, like a low-lying cloud or fog bank, faintly luminous, shot with fluorescent gleams. As the squadron drew nearer in its desperate charge, the separate forms of the troopers shaped themselves, and the galloping guardsmen grew ghastly with supernatural splendor.

Although I knew them to be immaterial and without mass or weight, I was terrified at their approach, fearing to be swept under the hoofs of the nightmares they rode. Like one in a dream, I started to run, but in another instant they were upon me, and I turned on my stream of formaldybrom. Then I was overwhelmed by a cloudburst of wild warlike wraiths.

The column swept past me, over the bank, plunging to its historic fate. The cut was piled full of frenzied, scrambling specters, as rank after rank swept down into the horrid gut. At last, the ditch swarmed full of writhing forms, and the carnage was dire.

My assistants with the extinguishers stood firm, and although almost unnerved by the sight, they summoned their courage, and directed simultaneous streams of formaldybrom into the struggling mass of fantoms. As soon as my mind returned, I busied myself with the huge tanks I had prepared for use as receivers. These were fitted with a mechanism similar to that employed in portable forges, by which the heavy vapor was sucked off. Luckily, the night was calm, and I was able to fill a dozen cylinders with the precipitated ghosts. The segregation of individual forms was, of course, impossible, so that men and horses were mingled in a horrible mixture of fricasseed spirits. I intended subsequently to empty the soup into a large reservoir and allow the separate specters to reform according to the laws of spiritual cohesion.

Circumstances, however, prevented me from accomplishing this result. I returned home to find awaiting me an order so large and important that I had no time in which to operate upon my cylinders of cavalry.

My patron was the proprietor of a new sanatorium for nervous invalids, located near some medicinal springs in the Catskills. His building was unfortunately located, having been built upon the site of a once-famous summer hotel, which, while filled with guests, had burned to the ground, resulting in scores of lives being lost. Just before the patients were to be installed in the new structure, it was found that the place was haunted by the victims of the conflagration to a degree that rendered it inconvenient as a health resort. My professional services were requested, therefore, to render the building a fitting abode for convalescents. I wrote to the proprietor, fixing my charge at five thousand dollars. As my usual rate was one hundred dollars per ghost, and over a hundred lives were lost at the fire, I considered this price reasonable, and my offer was accepted.

The sanatorium job was finished in a week. I secured one hundred and two superior spectral specimens, and upon my return to the laboratory, I put them up in heavily embossed tins with attractive labels in colors.

My delight at the outcome of this business was, however, soon transformed into anger and indignation. The proprietor of the health resort, having found that the specters from his place had been sold, claimed a rebate upon the contract price equal to the value of the modified ghosts transferred to my possession. This, of course, I could not allow. I wrote, demanding immediate payment according to our agreement, and this was peremptorily refused. The manager's letter was insulting in the extreme. The Pied Piper of Hamelin was not worse treated than I felt myself to be; so, like the piper, I was determined to have my revenge.

I got out the twelve tanks of Waterloo ghost-hash from the storerooms and treated them with radium for two days. These I shipped to the Catskills billed as hydrogen gas. Then, accompanied by two trustworthy assistants, I went to the sanatorium and preferred my demand for payment in person. I was ejected with contempt. Before my hasty exit, however, I had the satisfaction of noticing that the building was filled with patients. Languid ladies were seated in wicker chairs upon the piazzas, and frail, anemic girls filled the corridors. It was a hospital of nervous wrecks, whom the slightest disturbance would throw into a panic. I suppressed all my finer feelings of mercy and kindness and smiled grimly as I walked back to the village.

That night was black and lowering, fitting weather for the pandemonium I was about to turn loose. At ten o'clock, I loaded a wagon with the tanks of compressed cohorts, and, muffled in heavy overcoats, we drove to the sanatorium. All was silent as we approached; all was dark. When the wagon concealed in a grove of pines, we took out the tanks one by one, and placed them beneath the ground-floor windows. The sashes were easily forced open, and raised enough to enable us to insert the rubber tubes connected with the iron reservoirs. At midnight, everything was ready.

I gave the word, and my assistants ran from tank to tank, opening the stopcocks. With a hiss as of escaping steam, the huge vessels emptied themselves, vomiting forth clouds of vapor, which, upon contact with the air, coagulated into strange shapes as the white of an egg does when dropped into boiling water. The rooms became instantly filled with dismembered shades of men and horses seeking wildly to unite themselves with their proper parts.

Legs ran down the corridors, seeking their respective trunks; arms writhed wildly, reaching for missing bodies, heads rolled hither and yon in search of native necks. Horses' tails and hoofs whisked and hurried in quest of equine ownership until, reorganized, the spectral steeds galloped about to find their riders.

Had it been possible, I would have stopped this riot of wraiths long before this, for it was more awful than I had anticipated, but it was already too late. Cowering in the garden, I began to hear the screams of awakened and distracted patients. In another moment, the front door of the hotel burst open, and a mob of hysterical women in expensive nightgowns rushed out onto the lawn, and huddled in shrieking groups.

I fled into the night.

I fled, but Napoleon's men fled with me. Compelled by I know not what fatal astral attraction, perhaps the subtle affinity of the creature for the creator, the spectral shells, moved by some mysterious mechanics of a spiritual being, pursued me with fatuous fury.

I sought refuge, first, in my laboratory, but, even as I approached, a lurid glare foretold me of its destruction.

As I drew nearer, the whole ghost-factory was seen to be in flames; every moment, crackling reports were heard, as the overheated tins of phantasmagoria exploded and threw their supernatural contents upon the night.

These liberated ghosts joined the army of Napoleon's outraged warriors, and turned upon me.

There was not enough formaldybrom in all the world to quench their fierce energy. There was no place in all the world safe for me from their visitation. No ghost-extinguisher was powerful enough to lay the host of spirits that haunted me henceforth, and I had neither time nor money left with which to construct new Gatling quick-firing tanks.

It is little comfort to me to know that one hundred nervous invalids were completely restored to health by means of the terrific shock that I administered.

Doom of the House of Duryea
by Earl Peirce, Jr. 1936

I.

Arthur Duryea, a young, handsome man, came to meet his father for the first time in twenty years. As he strode into the hotel lobby – with long strides that had the spring of elastic in them – idle eyes lifted to appraise him, for he was an impressive figure, somehow grim with exaltation.

The desk clerk looked up with his habitual smile of expectation, how-do-you-do-Mr.-so-and-so, and his fingers strayed to the green fountain pen that stood in a holder on the desk.

Arthur Duryea cleared his throat, but still, his voice was clogged and unsteady. To the clerk, he said:

»I'm looking for my father, Doctor Henry Duryea. I understand he is registered here. He has recently arrived from Paris.«

The clerk lowered his gaze to a list of names. »Doctor Duryea is in Suite 600, sixth floor«. He looked up, his eyebrows arched questioningly. »Are you staying too, sir, Mr. Duryea?«

Arthur took the pen and scribbled his name rapidly. Without a further word, neglecting even to get his key and own room number, he turned and walked to the elevators. Not until he reached his father's suite on the sixth floor did he make an audible noise, and this was a mere sigh that fell from his lips like a prayer.

The man who opened the door was unusually tall, his slender frame clothed in tight-fitting black. He hardly dared to smile. His clean-shaven face was pale, an almost livid whiteness against the sparkle in his eyes. His jaw had a bluish luster.

»Arthur!« The word was scarcely a whisper. It seemed choked up quietly, as if it had been repeated time and again on his thin lips.

Arthur Duryea felt the kindliness of those eyes go through him, and then he was in his father's embrace.

Later, when these two grown men had regained their outer calm, they closed the door and went into the drawing-room. The elder Duryea held out a humidor of fine cigars, and his hand shook so hard when he held the match that his son was forced to cup his own hands about the flame. They both had tears in their eyes, but their eyes were smiling.

Henry Duryea placed a hand on his son's shoulder. »This is the happiest day of my life«, he said. »You can never know how much I have longed for this moment.«

Arthur, looking into that glance, realized, with growing pride, that he had loved his father all his life, despite any of those things that had been cursed against him. He sat down on the edge of a chair.

»I – I don't know how to act«, he confessed. »You surprise me, Dad. You're so different from what I had expected.«

A cloud came over Doctor Duryea's features. »What did you expect, Arthur?«, he demanded quickly. »An evil eye? A shaven head and knotted jowls?«

»Please, Dad – no!« Arthur's words clipped short. »I don't think I ever really visualized you. I knew you would be a splendid man. But I thought you'd look older, more like a man who has really suffered.«

»I have suffered more than I can ever describe. But seeing you again and the prospect of spending the rest of my life with you has more than compensated for my sorrows. Even during the twenty years we were apart, I found an ironic joy in learning of your progress in college, and in your American game of football.«

»Then you've been following my work?«

»Yes, Arthur; I've received monthly reports ever since you left me. From my study in Paris, I've been really close to you, working out your problems as if they were my own. And now that the twenty years are completed, the ban that kept us apart is lifted forever. From now on, son, we shall be the closest of companions – unless your Aunt Cecilia has succeeded in her terrible mission.«

The mention of that name caused an unfamiliar chill to come between the two men. It stood for something, in each of them, which gnawed their minds like a malignancy. But to the younger Duryea, in his intense effort to forget the awful past, her name as well as her madness must be forgotten.

He had no wish to carry on this subject of conversation, for it betrayed an internal weakness that he hated. With forced determination and a ludicrous lift of his eyebrows, he said:

»Cecilia is dead, and her silly superstition is dead too. From now on, Dad, we're going to enjoy life as we should. Bygones are really bygones in this case.«

Doctor Duryea closed his eyes slowly, as though an exquisite pain had gone through him.

»Then you have no indignation?«, he questioned. »You have none of your aunt's hatred?«

»Indignation? Hatred?« Arthur laughed aloud. »Ever since I was twelve years old, I have disbelieved Cecilia's stories. I have known that those horrible things were impossible, that they belonged to the ancient category of mythology and tradition. How, then, can I be indignant, and how can I hate you? How can I do anything but recognize Cecilia for what she was – a mean, frustrated woman, cursed with an insane grudge against you and your family? I tell you, Dad, that nothing she has ever said can possibly come between us again.«

Henry Duryea nodded his head. His lips were tight together, and the muscles in his throat held back a cry. In that same soft tone of defense, he spoke further, doubting words.

»Are you so sure of your subconscious mind, Arthur? Can you be so certain that you are free from all suspicion, however vague? Is there not a lingering premonition – premonition that warns of peril?«

»No, Dad – no!« Arthur shot to his feet. »I don't believe it. I've never believed it. I know, as any sane man would know, that you are neither a vampire nor a murderer. You know it too, and Cecilia knew it, only she was mad.«

»That family rot is dispelled, Father. This is a civilized century. Belief in vampirism is sheer lunacy. Wh – why, it's too absurd even to think about!«

»You have the enthusiasm of youth«, said his father in a rather tired voice. »But have you not heard the legend?«

Arthur stepped back instinctively. He moistened his lips, for their dryness might crack them. »The – legend?«

He said the word in a curious hush of awed softness, as he had heard his aunt Cecilia say it many times before.

»That awful legend that you – – «

»That I eat my children?«

»Oh, God, Father!« Arthur went to his knees as a cry burst through his lips. »Dad, that – that's ghastly! We must forget Cecilia's ravings.«

»You are affected, then?«, asked Doctor Duryea bitterly.

»Affected? Certainly I'm affected, but only as I should be at such an accusation. Cecilia was mad, I tell you. Those books she showed me years ago, and those folktales of vampires and ghouls – they burned into my infantile mind like acid. They haunted me day and night in my youth and caused me to hate you worse than death itself.«

»But in Heaven's name, Father, I've outgrown those things as I have outgrown my clothes. I'm a man now; do you understand that? A man, with a man's sense of logic.«

»Yes, I understand.« Henry Duryea threw his cigar into the fireplace, and placed a hand on his son's shoulder.

»We shall forget Cecilia«, he said. »As I told you in my letter, I have rented a lodge in Maine where we can go to be alone for the rest of the summer. We'll get in some fishing and hiking, and perhaps some hunting. But first, Arthur, I must be sure in my own mind that you are sure of yours. I must be sure you won't bar your door against me at night, and sleep with a loaded revolver at your elbow. I must be sure that you're not afraid of going up there alone with me, and dying – – «

His voice ended abruptly, as if an age-long dread had taken hold of it. His son's face was waxen, with sweat standing out like pearls on his brow. He said nothing, but his eyes were filled with questions that his lips could not put into words. His own hand touched his father's, and tightened over it.

Henry Duryea drew his hand away.

»I'm sorry«, he said, and his eyes looked straight over Arthur's lowered head. »This thing must be thrashed out now. I believe you when you say that you discredit Cecilia's stories, but for sake greater than sanity, I must tell you the truth behind the legend – and believe me, Arthur, there is a truth!«

He climbed to his feet and walked to the window, which looked out over the street below. For a moment, he gazed into space, silent. Then he turned and looked down at his son.

»You have heard only your aunt's version of the legend, Arthur. Doubtless, it was warped into something far more hideous than it actually was – if that is possible! Doubtless she spoke to you of the Inquisitorial stake in Carcassonne, where one of my ancestors perished. Also, she may have mentioned that book, Vampires, which a former Duryea is supposed to have written. Then certainly she told you about your two younger brothers – my own poor, motherless children – who were sucked bloodlessly in their cradles ... «

Arthur Duryea passed a hand across his aching eyes. Those words, so often repeated by that witch of an aunt, stirred up the same visions that had made his childhood nights sleepless with terror. He could hardly bear to hear them again – and from the very man to whom they were accredited.

»Listen, Arthur«, the elder Duryea went on quickly, his voice low with the pain it gave him. »You must know the true basis of your aunt's hatred. You must know of that curse – that curse of vampirism which is supposed to have followed the Duryeas through five centuries of French history but which we can dispel as pure superstition, so often connected with ancient families. But I must tell you that this part of the legend is true:«

»Your two young brothers actually died in their cradles, bloodless. And I stood trial in France for their murder, and my name was smirched throughout all of Europe with such an inhuman damnation that it drove your aunt and you to America, and has left me childless, hated, and ostracized from society the world over.«

»I must tell you that on that terrible night in Duryea Castle, I had been working late on historic volumes of Crespet and Prinn, and on that loathsome tome, Vampires. I must tell you of the soreness that was in my throat and of the heaviness of the blood that coursed through my veins ... And of that presence, which was neither man nor animal, but which I knew was some place near me, yet neither within the castle nor outside of it, and which was closer to me than my heart and more terrible to me than the touch of the grave ... «

»I was at the desk in my library, my head swimming in a delirium that left me senseless until dawn. There were nightmares that frightened me – frightened me, Arthur, a grown man who had dissected countless cadavers in morgues and medical schools. I know that my tongue was swollen in my mouth, that brine moistened my lips, and that rottenness pervaded my body like a fever.«

»I can make no recollection of sanity or of consciousness. That night remains vivid, unforgettable, yet somehow completely in shadows. When I had fallen asleep – if in God's name it was sleep – I was slumped across my desk. But when I awoke in the morning, I was lying face down on my couch. So you see, Arthur, I had moved during that night, and I had never known it!«

»What I'd done and where I'd gone during those dark hours will always remain an impenetrable mystery. But I do know this. On the morrow, I was torn from my sleep by the shrieks of maids and butlers and by the mad wailing of your aunt. I stumbled through the open door of my study, and in the nursery I saw those two babies there – lifeless, white and dry like mummies, and with twin holes in their necks that were caked black with their own blood ... «

»Oh, I don't blame you for your incredulousness, Arthur. I cannot believe it yet myself, nor shall I ever believe it. The belief in it would drive me to suicide, and still, the doubting of it drives me mad with horror.«

»All of France was doubtful, and even the savants who defended my name at the trial found that they could not explain it nor disbelieve it. The case was quieted by the Republic, for it might have shaken science to its very foundation and split the pedestals of religion and logic. I was released from the charge of murder, but the actual murder has hung about me like a stench.«

»The coroners who examined those tiny cadavers found them both dry of all their blood, but could find no blood on the floor of the nursery nor in the cradles. Something from hell stalked the halls of Duryea that night – and I should blow my brains out if I dared to think deeply of what that was. You, too, my son, would have been dead and bloodless if you hadn't been sleeping in a separate room with your door barred on the inside.«

»You were a timid child, Arthur. You were only seven years old, but you were filled with the folklore of those mad Lombards and the decadent poetry of your aunt. On that same night, while I was somewhere between heaven and hell, you also heard the padded footsteps on the stone corridor and the tugging at your door handle, for in the morning you complained of a chill and of terrible nightmares that frightened you in your sleep ... I only thank God that your door was barred!«

Henry Duryea's voice choked into a sob, which brought the stinging tears back into his eyes. He paused to wipe his face, and to dig his fingers into his palm.

»You understand, Arthur, that for twenty years, under my sworn oath at the Palace of Justice, I could neither see you nor write to you. Twenty years, my son, while all of that time you had grown to hate me and to spit at my name. Not until your aunt's death have you called yourself a Duryea ... And now you come to me at my bidding, and say you love me as a son should love his father.«

»Perhaps it is God's forgiveness for everything. Now, at last, we shall be together, and that terrible, unexplainable past will be buried for ever ... «

He put his handkerchief back into his pocket and walked slowly to his son. He dropped to one knee, and his hands gripped Arthur's arms.

»My son, I can say no more to you. I have told you the truth, as I alone know it. I may be, by all accounts, some ghoulish creation of Satan on earth. I may be a child-killer, a vampire or some morbidly diseased specimen of vrykolakas–things that science cannot explain.«

»Perhaps the dreaded legend of the Duryeas is true. Autiel Duryea was convicted of murdering his brother in that same monstrous fashion in the year 1576, and he died in flames at the stake. François Duryea, in 1802, blew his head apart with a blunderbuss on the morning after his youngest son was found dead, apparently from anemia. And there are others, of whom I cannot bear to speak, that would chill your soul if you were to hear them.«

»So you see, Arthur, there is a hellish tradition behind our family. There is a heritage that no sane God would ever have allowed. The future of the Duryeas lies in you, for you are the last of the race. I pray with all of my heart that Providence will permit you to live your full share of years, and to leave other Duryeas behind you. And so if ever again I feel that presence as I did in Duryea Castle, I am going to die as François Duryea died, over a hundred years ago ... «

He stood up, and his son stood up at his side.

»If you are willing to forget, Arthur, we shall go up to that lodge in Maine. There is a life we've never known awaiting us. We must find that life, and we must find the happiness that a curious fate snatched from us on those Lombard sour lands twenty years ago ... «

II.

Henry Duryea's tall stature, coupled with a slenderness of frame and a sleekness of muscle, gave him an appearance that was unusually gaunt. His son couldn't help but think of that word as he sat on the rustic porch of the lodge, watching his father sunning himself at the lake's edge.

Henry Duryea had a kindliness in his face, at times an almost sublime kindliness, which great prophets often possess. But when his face was partly in shadows, particularly about his brow, there was a frightening tone that came into his features; for it was a tone of farness, of mysticism, and conjuration. Somehow, in the late evenings, he assumed the unapproachable mantle of a dreamer and sat silently before the fire, his mind ever off in unknown places.

In that little lodge, there was no electricity, and the glow of the oil lamps played curious tricks with human expression which frequently resulted in something unhuman. It may have been the dusk of night, the flickering of the lamps, but Arthur Duryea had certainly noticed how his father's eyes had sunken further into his head, how his cheeks were tighter, and how the outline of his teeth pressed into the skin about his lips.

It was nearing sundown on the second day of their stay at Timber Lake. Six miles away, the dirt road wound on toward Houtlon, near the Canadian border. So it was lonely there, on a solitary little lake hemmed in closely with dark evergreens and a sky that drooped low over dusty-summited mountains.

Within the lodge was a cozy fireplace and a glossy elk's-head that peered out above the mantel. There were guns and fishing tackle on the walls, shelves of reliable American fiction – Mark Twain, Melville, Stockton, and a well-worn edition of Bret Harte.

A fully supplied kitchen and a wood stove furnished them with hearty meals, which were welcome after a whole day's tramp in the woods. On that evening, Henry Duryea prepared a select French stew out of every available vegetable, and a can of soup. They ate well, then stretched out before the fire for a smoke. They were outlining a trip to the Orient together, when the back door blew open with a terrific bang, and a wind swept into the lodge with a coldness that chilled them both.

»A storm«, Henry Duryea said, rising to his feet. »Sometimes they have them up here, and they're pretty bad. The roof might leak over your bedroom. Perhaps you'd like to sleep down here with me.« His fingers strayed playfully over his son's head as he went out into the kitchen to bar the swinging door.

Arthur's room was upstairs, next to a spare room filled with extra furniture. He'd chosen it because he liked the altitude and because the only other bedroom was occupied ...

He went upstairs swiftly and silently. His roof didn't leak; it was absurd even to think it might. It had been his father again, suggesting that they sleep together. He had done it before, in a jesting, whispering way–as if to challenge them both if they dared to sleep together.

Arthur came back downstairs, dressed in his bathrobe and slippers. He stood on the fifth stair, rubbing a two-day's growth of beard. »I think I'll shave tonight«, he said to his father. »May I use your razor?«

Henry Duryea, draped in a black raincoat and with his face haloed in the brim of a rainhat, looked up from the hall. A frown glided obscurely from his features. »Not at all, son. Sleeping upstairs?«

Arthur nodded, and quickly said, »Are you – going out?«

»Yes, I'm going to tie the boats up tighter. I'm afraid the lake will rough it up a bit.«

Duryea jerked back the door and stepped outside. The door slammed shut, and his footsteps sounded on the wood flooring of the porch.

Arthur came slowly down the remaining steps. He saw his father's figure pass across the dark rectangle of a window, saw the flash of lightning that suddenly printed his grim silhouette against the glass.

He sighed deeply, a sigh that burned in his throat; for his throat was sore and aching. Then he went into the bedroom, found the razor lying in plain view on a birch tabletop.

As he reached for it, his glance fell upon his father's open Gladstone bag that rested at the foot of the bed. There was a book resting there, half hidden by a gray flannel shirt. It was a narrow, yellow-bound book, oddly out of place.

Frowning, he bent down and lifted it from the bag. It was surprisingly heavy in his hands, and he noticed a faintly sickening odor of decay that drifted from it like a perfume. The title of the volume had been thumbed away into an indecipherable blur of gold letters. But pasted across the front cover was a white strip of paper, on which was typewritten the word – INFANTIPHAGI.

He flipped back the cover and ran his eyes over the title-page. The book was printed in French – an early French – yet to him wholly comprehensible. The publication date was 1580, in Caen.

Breathlessly, he turned back a second page, saw a chapter headed, Vampires.

He slumped to one elbow across the bed. His eyes were four inches from those mildewed pages and his nostrils reeked with the stench of them.

He skipped long paragraphs of pedantic jargon on theology, he scanned brief accounts of strange, blood-eating monsters, vrykolakes, and leprechauns. He read of Jeanne d'Arc, of Ludvig Prinn, and muttered aloud the Latin snatches from Episcopi.

He passed pages in quick succession, his fingers shaking with the fear of it and his eyes hanging heavily in their sockets. He saw a vague reference to 'Enoch', and saw the terrible drawings by an ancient Dominican of Rome ...

Paragraph after paragraph, he read: the horror-striking testimony of Nider's Ant-Hill, the testimony of people who died shrieking at the stake; the recitals of grave-tenders, of jurists, and hangmen. Then unexpectedly, among all of this monumental vestige, there appeared before his eyes the name of – Autie Duryea, and he stopped reading as though invisibly struck.

Thunder clapped near the lodge and rattled the window-panes. The deep rolling of bursting clouds echoed over the valley. But he heard none of it. His eyes were on those two short sentences that his father – someone – had underlined with dark red crayon.

... The execution of Autiel Duryea three years ago does not end the Duryea controversy. Time alone can decide whether the Demon has claimed that family from its beginning to its end ...

Arthur read on about the trial of Autiel Duryea before Veniti, the Carcassonnean Inquisitor-General; he read, with mounting horror, the evidence that had sent that far-gone Duryea to the pillar – the evidence of a bloodless corpse who had been Autiel Duryea's young brother.

Unmindful now of the tremendous storm that had centered over Timber Lake, unheeding the clatter of windows and the swish of pines on the roof – even of his father, who worked down at the lake's edge in a drenching rain – Arthur fastened his glance to the blurred print of those pages, sinking deeper and deeper into the garbled legends of a dark age ...

On the last page of the chapter, he again saw the name of his ancestor, Autiel Duryea. He traced a shaking finger over the narrow lines of words, and when he finished reading them, he rolled sideways on the bed, and from his lips came a sobbing, mumbling prayer.

»God, oh God in Heaven protect me ... «

For he had read:

'As in the case of Autiel Duryea, we observe that this specimen of vrykolakas preys only upon the blood of its own family. It possesses none of the characteristics of the undead vampire, being usually a living male person of otherwise normal appearances, unsuspecting its inherent demonism.'

'But this vrykolakas cannot act according to its demoniacal possession unless it is in the presence of a second member of the same family, who acts as a medium between the man and its demon. This medium has none of the traits of the vampire, but it senses the being of this creature (when the metamorphosis is about to occur) by reason of intense pains in the head and throat. Both the vampire and the medium undergo similar reactions, involving nausea, nocturnal visions, and physical disquietude.'

'When these two outcasts are within a certain distance of each other, the coalescence of inherent demonism is completed, and the vampire is subject to its attacks, demanding blood for its sustenance. No member of the family is safe at these times, for the vrykolakas, acting in their true agency on earth, will unerringly seek out the blood. In rare cases where other victims are unavailable, the vampire will even take the blood from the very medium that made it possible.'

'This vampire is born into certain aged families, and naught but death can destroy it. It is not conscious of its blood-madness, and acts only in a psychic state. The medium, too, is unaware of its terrible role; and when these two are together, despite any lapse of years, the fusion of inheritance is so violent that no power known on earth can turn it back.'

III.

The lodge door slammed shut with a sudden, interrupting bang. The lock grated, and Henry Duryea's footsteps sounded on the planked floor.

Arthur shook himself off the bed. He had only time to fling that haunting book into the Gladstone bag before he sensed his father standing in the doorway.

»You – you're not shaving, Arthur.« Duryea's words, spliced hesitantly, were toneless. He glanced from the tabletop to the Gladstone and to his son. He said nothing for a moment, his glance inscrutable. Then he said:

»It's blowing up quite a storm outside.«

Arthur swallowed the first words that had come into his throat and nodded quickly. »Yes, isn't it? Quite a storm.« He met his father's gaze, his face burning. »I – I don't think I'll shave, Dad. My head aches.«

Duryea came swiftly into the room and pinned Arthur's arms in his grasp. »What do you mean – your head aches? How? Does your throat – – «

»No!« Arthur jerked himself away. He laughed. »It's that French stew of yours! It's hit me in the stomach!« He stepped past his father and started up the stairs.

»The stew?« Duryea pivoted on his heel. »Possibly. I think I feel it myself.«

Arthur stopped, his face suddenly white. »You – too?«

The words were hardly audible. Their glances met – clashed like dueling-swords.

For ten seconds, neither of them said a word or moved a muscle: Arthur, from the stairs, looking down; his father below, gazing up at him. In Henry Duryea, the blood drained slowly from his face and left a purple etching across the bridge of his nose and above his eyes. He looked like a death's-head.

Arthur winced at the sight and twisted his eyes away. He turned to go up the remaining stairs.

»Son!«

He stopped again; his hand tightened on the banister.

»Yes, Dad?«

Duryea put his foot on the first stair and said, »I want you to lock your door tonight. The wind would keep it banging!«

»Yes«, breathed Arthur, and he pushed up the stairs to his room.

Doctor Duryea's hollow footsteps sounded in steady, unhesitant beats across the floor of Timber Lake Lodge. Sometimes they stopped, and the crackling hiss of a sulfur match took their place, then perhaps a distended sigh, and, again, footsteps …

Arthur crouched at the open door of his room. His head was cocked for those noises from below. In his hands was a double-barrel shotgun of violent gage.

… thud … thud … thud …

Then a pause, the clinking of a glass, and the gurgling of liquid. The sigh, the tread of his feet over the floor ...

'He's thirsty', Arthur thought – 'thirsty!'

Outside, the storm had grown into fury. Lightning zigzagged between the mountains, filling the valley with weird phosphorescence. Thunder, like drums, rolled incessantly.

Within the lodge, the heat of the fireplace piled the atmosphere thick with stagnation. All the doors and windows were locked shut and the oil-lamps glowed weakly – a pale, anemic light.

Henry Duryea walked to the foot of the stairs and stood, looking up.

Arthur sensed his movements, he dodged an went back into his room, the gun gripped in his shaking fingers.

Then Henry Duryea's footstep sounded on the first stair.

Arthur slumped to one knee. He buckled a fist against his teeth as a prayer tumbled through them.

Duryea climbed a second step ... and another ... and still one more. On the fourth stair, he stopped.

»Arthur!« His voice cut into the silence like the crack of a whip. »Arthur! Will you come down here?«

»Yes, Dad.« Bedraggled, his body hanging like cloth, young Duryea took five steps to the landing.

»We can't be zanies!« cried Henry Duryea. »My soul is sick with dread. Tomorrow, we're going back to New York. I'm going to get the first boat to open sea ... Please come down here.« He turned around and descended the stairs to his room.

Arthur choked back the words that had lumped in his mouth. Half dazed, he followed ...

In the bedroom, he saw his father stretched face-up along the bed. He saw a pile of rope at his father's feet.

»Tie me to the bedposts, Arthur«, came the command. »Tie both my hands and both my feet.«

Arthur stood gaping.

»Do as I tell you!«

»Dad, what hor – – «

»Don't be a fool! You read that book! You know what relation you are to me! I'd always hoped it was Cecilia, but now I know it's you. I should have known it on that night twenty years ago when you complained of a headache and nightmares ... Quickly, my head rocks with pain. Tie me!«

Speechless, his own pain piercing him with agony, Arthur fell to that grisly task. Both hands he tied – and both feet ... he tied them so firmly to the iron posts that his father could not lift himself an inch off the bed.

Then he blew out the lamps, and without a further glance at that Prometheus, he reascended the stairs to his room and slammed and locked his door behind him. He looked once at the breech of his gun and set it against a chair by his bed. He flung off his robe and slippers, and within five minutes he was senseless in slumber.

IV.

He slept late, and when he awakened, his muscles were as stiff as boards, and the lingering visions of a nightmare clung before his eyes. He pushed his way out of bed and stood dazedly on the floor.

A dull, numbing torture circulated through his head. He felt bloated ... coarse, and running with internal mucus. His mouth was dry and his gums were sore and stinging.

He tightened his hands as he lunged for the door. »Dad«, he cried, and he heard his voice breaking in his throat.

Sunlight filtered through the window at the top of the stairs. The air was hot and dry and carried in it a mild odor of decay.

Arthur suddenly drew back at that odor – drew back with a gasp of awful fear. For he recognized it – that stench, the heaviness of his blood, the rawness of his tongue and gums ... Age-long it seemed, yet rising like a spirit in his memory. All of these things he had known and felt before.

He leaned against the banister, and half slid, half stumbled down the stairs ...

His father had died during the night. He lay like a waxen figure tied to his bed, his face done up in knots.

»He lay like a waxen figure tied to his bed, unable to move, tied to the bed as he had firmly fixed him the night before.«

Arthur stood dumbly at the foot of the bed for only a few seconds; then he went back upstairs to his room.

Almost immediately, he emptied both barrels of the shotgun into his head.

The tragedy at Timber Lake was discovered accidentally three days later. A party of fishermen, upon finding the two bodies, notified state authorities, and an investigation was directly underway.

Arthur Duryea had undoubtedly met death at his own hands. The condition of his wounds and the manner in which he held the lethal weapon, at once foreclosed the suspicion of any foul play.

But the death of Doctor Henry Duryea confronted the police with an inexplicable mystery; for his trussed-up body, unscathed except for two jagged holes over the jugular vein, had been drained of all its blood.

The autopsy protocol of Henry Duryea laid death to 'undetermined causes', and it was not until the yellow tabloids commenced an investigation into the Duryea family history that the incredible and fantastic explanations were offered to the public.

Obviously, such talk was held in popular contempt; yet in view of the controversial war which followed, the authorities considered it expedient to consign both Duryeas to the crematory ...

THE VOICE OF THE NIGHT
by by William Hope Hodgson (1907)

I.

It was a dark, starless night. We were becalmed in the Northern Pacific. Our exact position I do not know, for the sun had been hidden during the course of a weary, breathless week by a thin haze that had seemed to float above us, about the height of our mastheads, at times descending and shrouding the surrounding sea.

With there being no wind, we had steadied the tiller, and I was the only man on deck. The crew, consisting of two men and a boy, were sleeping orward in their den, while Will – my friend and the master of our little craft – was aft in his bunk on the port side of the little cabin.

Suddenly, from out of the surrounding darkness, there came a hail: »Schooner, ahoy!«

The cry was so unexpected that I gave no immediate answer, because of my surprise.

It came again – a voice curiously throaty and inhuman, calling from somewhere upon the dark sea away on our port broadside:

»Schooner, ahoy!«

»Hullo!«, I sung out, having gathered my wits somewhat. »What are you? What do you want?«

»You need not be afraid«, answered the queer voice, having probably noticed some trace of confusion in my tone. »I am only an old – man.«

The pause sounded odd, but it was only afterward that it came back to me with any significance.

»Why don't you come alongside, then?«, I queried somewhat snappishly; for I liked not his hinting at my having been a trifle shaken.

»I – I – can't. It wouldn't be safe. I – « The voice broke off, and there was silence.

»What do you mean?«, I asked, growing more and more astonished.

»What's not safe? Where are you?«

I listened for a moment, but there came no answer. And then, with a sudden, indefinite suspicion of I knew not what coming to me, I stepped swiftly to the binnacle and took out the lighted lamp. At the same time, I knocked on the deck with my heel to wake up Will. Then I was back at the side, throwing the yellow funnel of light out into the silent immensity beyond our rail. As I did so I heard a slight muffled cry, and then the sound of a splash, as though someone had dipped

103

oars abruptly. Yet I cannot say with certainty that I saw anything; save, it seemed to me, that with the first flash of the light, there had been something upon the waters, where now there was nothing.

»Hullo, there!«, I called. »What foolery is this?«

But there came only the indistinct sounds of a boat being pulled away into the night.

Then I heard Will's voice from the direction of the after scuttle:

»What's up, George?«

»Come here. Will!«, I said.

»What is it?«, he asked, coming across the deck.

I told him the queer thing that had happened. He asked several questions; then, after a moment's silence, he raised his hands to his lips and hailed:

»Boat, ahoy!«

From a long distance away, there came back to us a faint reply, and my companion repeated his call. Presently, after a short period of silence, there grew on our hearing the muffled sound of oars, at which Will hailed again.

This time there was a reply: »Put away the light.«

»I'm damned if I will«, I muttered; but Will told me to do as the voice bade, and I shoved it down under the bulwarks.

»Come nearer«, he said, and the oar strokes continued. Then, when apparently some half-dozen fathoms distant, they again ceased.

»Come alongside!«, exclaimed Will. »There's nothing to be frightened of aboard here.«

»Promise that you will not show the light?«

»What has that to do with you«, I burst out, »that you're so infernally afraid of the light?«

»Because – «, began the voice, and stopped short.

»Because what?«, I asked quickly.

Will put his hand on my shoulder. »Shut up a minute, old man«, he said, in a low voice. »Let me tackle him.«

He leaned more over the rail.

»See here, mister«, he said, »this is a pretty queer business, you coming upon us like this, right out in the middle of the blessed Pacific. How are we to know what sort of hanky-panky trick you're up to? You say there's only one of you. How are we to know, unless we get a squint at you – eh? What's your objection to the light, anyway?«

As he finished, I heard the noise of the oars again, and then the voice came; but now from a greater distance, and sounding extremely hopeless and pathetic.

»I am sorry – sorry! I would not have troubled you, only I am hungry, and – so is she.«

The voice died away, and the sound of the oars, dipping irregularly, was borne to us.

»Stop!«, sang out Will. »I don't want to drive you away. Come back!«

»We'll keep the light hidden if you don't like it.«

He turned to me:

»It's a damned queer rig, this; but I think there's nothing to be afraid of?«

There was a question in his tone, and I replied.

»No, I think the poor devil's been wrecked around here and gone crazy.«

The sound of the oars drew nearer.

»Shove that lamp back in the binnacle«, said Will; then he leaned over the rail and listened. I replaced the lamp and came back to his side.

The dipping of the oars ceased some dozen yards away.

»Won't you come alongside now?«, asked Will in an even voice. »I have had the lamp put back in the binnacle.«

»I – I cannot«, replied the voice. » I dare not come nearer. I dare not even pay you for the – the provisions.«

»That's all right«, said Will, and hesitated. »You're welcome to as much grub as you can take – « Again, he hesitated.

»You are very good!«, exclaimed the voice. »May God, who understands everything, reward you – It broke off huskily.

»The – the lady?«, said Will abruptly. »Is she – «

»I have left her behind on the island«, came the voice.

»What island?«, I cut in.

»I know not its name«, returned the voice. »I would to God – « it began, and checked itself as suddenly.

»Could we not send a boat for her?«, asked Will at this point.

»No!«, said the voice, with extraordinary emphasis. »My God! No!«

There was a moment's pause; then it added, in a tone that seemed like a merited reproach:

»It was because of our want that I ventured – because her agony tortured me.«

»I am a forgetful brute!«, exclaimed Will. »Just wait a minute, whoever you are, and I will bring you up something at once.«

In a couple of minutes, he was back again, and his arms were full of various edibles. He paused at the rail.

»Can't you come alongside for them?«, he asked.

»"No – I dare not«, replied the voice, and it seemed to me that in its tones I detected a note of stifled craving – as though the owner hushed a mortal desire. It came to me then, in a flash, that the poor old creature out there in the darkness was suffering for actual need for that which Will held in his arms, and yet, because of some unintelligible dread, he was refraining from dashing to the side of our schooner and receiving it. And with the lightning-like conviction came the knowledge that the Invisible was not mad but sanely facing some intolerable horror.

»Damn it. Will!«, I said, full of many feelings, over which predominated a vast sympathy. »Get a box. We must float off the stuff to him in it.«

This we did, propelling it away from the vessel, out into the darkness, by means of a boat hook. In a minute, a slight cry from the Invisible came to us, and we knew that he had secured the box.

A little later, he called out a farewell to us, and it was such a heartful a blessing that I am sure we were the better for it. Then, without more ado, we heard the ply of oars across the darkness.

»Pretty soon off«, remarked Will, with perhaps just a little sense of injury.

»Wait«, I replied. »I think somehow he'll come back. He must have been badly in need for that food.«

»And the lady«, said Will. For a moment, he was silent; then he continued:

»It's the queerest thing ever I've tumbled across since I've been fishing.«

»Yes«, I said, and fell to pondering.

And so the time slipped away – an hour, another, and still Will stayed with me, for the queer adventure had knocked all desire for sleep out of him.

The third hour was three parts through when we heard again the sound of oars across the silent ocean.

"Listen!" said Will, a low note of excitement in his voice.

»He's coming, just as I thought«, I muttered.

The dipping of the oars grew nearer, and I noted that the strokes were firmer and longer. The food had been needed.

They came to a stop a little distance off the broadside, and the queer voice came again to us through the darkness:

»Schooner, ahoy!«

»That you?«, asked Will.

»Yes«, replied the voice. »I left you suddenly, but – but there was great need.«

»The lady?«, questioned Will.

»The – lady is grateful now on earth. She will be more grateful soon in – in heaven.«

Will began to make some reply, in a puzzled voice; but became confused, and broke off short. I said nothing. I was wondering at the curious pauses, and, apart from my wonder, I was full of great sympathy.

The voice continued:

»We – she and I, have talked, as we shared the result of God's tenderness and yours – «

Will interposed, but without coherence.

»I beg of you not to – to belittle your deed of Christian charity this night«, said the voice. »Be sure that it has not escaped His notice.«

It stopped, and there was a full minute's silence. Then it came again:

»We have spoken together upon that which - which has befallen us.

We had thought to go out, without telling anyone of the terror that has come into our – lives. She is with me in believing that tonight's happenings are under a special ruling, and that it is God's wish that we should tell you all that we have suffered since – since – «

»Yes?«, said Will softly.

»Since the sinking of the Albatross.«

»Ah!«, I exclaimed involuntarily. »She left Newcastle for 'Frisco some six months ago and hasn't been heard of since.«

»Yes«, answered the voice. »But some few degrees to the North of the line, she was caught in a terrible storm, and dismasted. When the day came, it was found that she was leaking badly, and, presently, it falling to a calm, the sailors took to the boats, leaving – leaving a young lady – my fiancée – and myself upon the wreck.«

»We were below, gathering together a few of our belongings, when they left. They were entirely callous, through fear, and when we came up upon the decks, we saw them only as small shapes afar off upon the horizon. Yet we did not despair but set to work and constructed a small raft. Upon this, we put such few matters as it would hold, including a quantity of water and some ship's biscuit.«

»Then, the vessel being very deep in the water, we got ourselves onto the raft and pushed off.«

»It was later when I observed that we seemed to be in the way of some tide or current, which bore us from the ship at an angle, so that in the course of three hours, by my watch, her hull became invisible to our sight, her broken masts remaining in view for a somewhat longer period. Then, towards evening, it grew misty, and so through the night. The next day, we were still encompassed by the mist, with the weather remaining quiet.«

»For four days we drifted through this strange haze, until, on the evening of the fourth day, there grew in our ears the murmur of breakers at a distance. Gradually it became plainer, and, somewhat after midnight, it appeared to sound upon either hand at no very great space. The raft was raised upon a swell several times, and then we were in smooth water, and the noise of the breakers was behind.«

»When the morning came, we found that we were in a sort of great lagoon, but of this we noticed little at the time; for close before us, through the enshrouding mist, loomed the hull of a large sailing vessel. With one accord, we fell upon our knees and thanked God, for we thought that here was an end to our perils. We had much to learn.

»The raft drew near to the ship, and we shouted at them to take us aboard; but none answered. Presently the raft touched against the side of the vessel, and seeing a rope hanging downward, I seized it and began to climb. Yet I had much ado to make my way up because of a kind of grey lichenous fungus that had seized upon the rope and which blotched the side of the ship lividly.«

»I reached the rail and clambered over it onto the deck. Here I saw that the decks were covered, in great patches, with gray masses, some of them rising into nodules several feet in height, but at the time I thought less of this matter than of the possibility of there being people aboard the ship. I shouted, but no one answered. Then I went to the door below the poop deck. I opened it and peered in.«

»There was a great smell of staleness, so that I knew in a moment that nothing living was within, and with the knowledge, I shut the door quickly; for I felt suddenly lonely.«

»I went back to the side where I had scrambled up. My – my sweetheart was still sitting quietly on the raft. Seeing me look down, she called up to know whether there were any aboard the ship. I replied that the vessel had the appearance of having been long deserted, but that if she would wait a little, I would see whether there was anything in the shape of a ladder by which she could ascend to the deck.

Then we would make a search through the vessel together. A little later, on the opposite side of the decks, I found a rope side ladder. This I carried across, and a minute afterwards she was beside me.«

»Together, we explored the cabins and apartments in the after part of the ship; but nowhere was there any sign of life. Here and there, within the cabins themselves, we came across odd patches of that queer fungus, but this, as my sweetheart said, could be cleansed away.«

»In the end, having assured ourselves that the after portion of the vessel was empty, we picked our ways to the bows, between the ugly gray nodules of that strange growth; and here we made a further search, which told us that there was indeed none aboard but ourselves.«

»This being now beyond any doubt, we returned to the stern of the ship and proceeded to make ourselves as comfortable as possible.«

»Together, we cleared out and cleaned two of the cabins; and after that, I examined whether there was anything eatable in the ship. This I soon found was so, and thanked God in my heart for His goodness. In addition to this, I discovered the whereabouts of the fresh-water pump, and having fixed it, I found the water drinkable, though somewhat unpleasant to the taste.«

»For several days, we stayed aboard the ship, without attempting to get to the shore. We were busily engaged in making the place habitable. Yet even thus early, we became aware that our lot was even less to be desired than might have been imagined; for though, as a first step, we scraped away the odd patches of growth that studded the floors and walls of the cabins and saloon, yet they returned almost to their original size within the space of twenty-four hours, which not only discouraged us but gave us a feeling of vague unease.«

»Still we would not admit ourselves beaten, so set to work afresh, and not only scraped away the fungus but soaked the places where it had been with carbolic, a can-full of which I had found in the pantry.«

»Yet, by the end of the week, the growth had returned in full strength, and, in addition, it had spread to other places, as though our touching it had allowed germs from it to travel elsewhere. «

»On the seventh morning, my sweetheart woke to find a small patch of it growing on her pillow, close to her face. At that, she came to me as soon as she could get her garments upon her. I was in the galley at the time, lighting the fire for breakfast.«

»'Come here, John', she said, and led me aft. When I saw the thing upon her pillow I shuddered, and then and there we agreed to go right out of the ship and see whether we could not fare to make ourselves more comfortable ashore.«

»Hurriedly, we gathered together our few belongings, and even among these, I found that the fungus had been at work, for one of her shawls had a little lump of it growing near one edge. I threw the whole thing over the side without saying anything to her.«

»The raft was still alongside, but it was too clumsy to guide, and I lowered down a small boat that hung across the stern, and in this manner we made our way to the shore. Yet, as we drew near to it, I became gradually aware that here the vile fungus, which had driven us from the ship, was growing riot. In places, it rose into horrible, fantastic mounds, which seemed almost to quiver, as with a quiet life, when the wind blew across them.

Here and there it took on the form of vast fingers, and in others it just spread out flat and smooth, and treacherous. Odd places, it appeared as grotesque stunted trees, seeming extraordinarily kinked and gnarled-the whole quaking vilely at times.«

»At first, it seemed to us that there was no single portion of the surrounding shore that was not hidden beneath the masses of the hideous lichen; yet, in this, I found we were mistaken; for somewhat later, coasting along the shore at a little distance, we descried a smooth white patch of what appeared to be fine sand, and there we landed. It was not sand.

What it was, I do not know. All that I have observed is that upon it the fungus will not grow, while everywhere else, save where the sand-like earth wanders oddly, path-wise, amid the grey desolation of the lichen, there is nothing but that loathsome greyness.«

»It is difficult to make you understand how cheered we were to find one place that was absolutely free from the growth, and here we deposited our belongings.

Then we went back to the ship for such things as it seemed to us we should need. Among other matters, I managed to bring ashore with me one of the ship's sails, with which I constructed two small tents, which, though exceedingly rough-shaped, served the purposes for which they were intended.

In these we lived and stored our various necessities, and thus, for a matter of some four weeks, all went smoothly and without particular unhappiness. Indeed, I may say with much happiness – for – for we were together.«

»It was on the thumb of her right hand that the growth first showed. It was only a small circular spot, much like a little gray mole. My God! how the fear leaped to my heart when she showed me the place. We cleansed it, between us, washing it with carbolic soap and water. In the morning of the following day, she showed her hand to me again.

The gray warty thing had returned. For a little while, we looked at one another in silence. Then, still wordless, we started again to remove it. In the midst of the operation, she spoke suddenly.«

»'What's that on the side of your face, dear?' Her voice was sharp with anxiety. I put my hand up to feel.«

»'There! Under the hair by your ear. A little to the front a bit.' My finger rested upon the place, and then I knew.«

»'Let us get your thumb done first', I said. And she submitted, only because she was afraid to touch me until it was cleansed. I finished washing and disinfecting her thumb, and then she turned to my face.«

»After it was finished, we sat together and talked awhile of many things; for there had come into our lives sudden, very terrible thoughts.«

We were, all at once, afraid of something worse than death. We spoke of loading the boat with provisions and water and making our way out onto the sea, yet we were helpless, for many causes and – and the growth had already attacked us. We decided to stay. God would do with us what was His will. We would wait.«

II.

»A month, two months and three months passed, and the places grew somewhat, and there came others. Yet we fought so strenuously with the fear that its headway was but slow, comparatively speaking.«

»Occasionally, we ventured off to the ship for such stores as we needed. There, we found that the fungus grew persistently. One of the nodules on the main deck soon became as high as my head.«

»We had now given up all thought or hope of leaving the island. We had realized that it would be unallowable to go among healthy humans with the things from which we were suffering.«

»With this determination and knowledge in our minds, we knew that we should have to husband our food and water; for we did not know, at that time, but that we should possibly live for many years.«

»This reminds me that I have told you that I am an old man. Judged by years this is not so. But – but – «

He broke off; then continued somewhat abruptly:

»As I was saying, we knew that we should use care in the matter of food. But we had no idea then how little food there was left of which to take care. It was a week later that I made the discovery that all the other bread tanks – which I had supposed to be full – were empty, and that (beyond odd tins of vegetables and meat, and some other matters) we had nothing on which to depend, but the bread in the tank, which I had already opened.«

»After learning this, I bestirred myself to do what I could and set out to work at fishing in the lagoon, but with no success. At this, I was somewhat inclined to feel desperate until the thought came to me to try outside the lagoon, in the open sea.«

»Here, at times, I caught odd fish, but so infrequently that they proved of little help in keeping us from the hunger that threatened. It seemed to me that our deaths were likely to come from hunger, and not from the growth of the thing that had seized upon our bodies.«

»We were in this state of mind when the fourth month wore out. Then I made a very horrible discovery. One morning, a little before midday, I came off the ship with a portion of the biscuits that were left. In the mouth of her tent, I saw my sweetheart sitting, eating something.«

»'What is it, my dear?', I called out as I leaped ashore. Yet, on hearing my voice, she seemed confused and, turning, slyly threw something toward the edge of the little clearing. It fell short, and a vague suspicion having arisen within me, I walked across and picked it up.«

»It was a piece of the gray fungus.«

»As I went to her with it in my hand, she turned deadly pale, then a rose red.«

»I felt strangely dazed and frightened.«

»'My dear! My dear!'«, I said, and could say no more. Yet at my words, she broke down and cried bitterly. Gradually, as she calmed, I got from her the news that she had tried it the preceding day, and – and liked it. I got her to promise on her knees not to touch it again, however great our hunger. After she had promised, she told me that the desire for it had come suddenly and that, until the moment of desire, she had experienced nothing toward it but the most extreme repulsion.«

»Later in the day, feeling strangely restless and much shaken by the thing that I had discovered, I made my way along one of the twisted paths – formed by the white, sand-like substance – which led among the fungoid growth. I had, once before, ventured along there; but not to any great distance. This time, being involved in perplexing thought, I went much farther than hitherto.«

»Suddenly, I was called to myself by a queer, hoarse sound on my left. Turning quickly, I saw that there was movement among an extraordinarily shaped mass of fungus, close to my elbow. It was swaying uneasily, as though it possessed a life of its own. Abruptly, as I stared, the thought came to me that the thing had a grotesque resemblance to the figure of a distorted human creature. Even as the fancy flashed into my brain, there was a slight, sickening noise of tearing, and I saw that one of the branchlike arms was detaching itself from the surrounding gray masses and coming toward me.«

»The head of the thing – a shapeless gray ball inclined in my direction. I stood stupidly, and the vile arm brushed across my face. I gave out a frightened cry and ran back a few paces. There was a sweetish taste on my lips where the thing had touched me. I licked them, and was immediately filled with an inhuman desire. I turned and seized a mass of the fungus. Then more, and – more. I was insatiable.«

»In the midst of devouring, the remembrance of the morning's discovery swept into my mazed brain. It was sent by God. I dashed the fragment I held to the ground. Then, utterly wretched and feeling a dreadful guiltiness, I made my way back to the little encampment.«

»I think she knew, by some marvelous intuition that love must have given, so soon as she set eyes on me. Her quiet sympathy made it easier for me, and I told her of my sudden weakness, yet omitted to mention the extraordinary thing which had gone before. I desired to spare her all unnecessary terror.«

»But, for myself, I had added an intolerable knowledge to breed an incessant terror in my brain; for I doubted not but that I had seen the end of one of these men who had come to the island in the ship in the lagoon; and in that monstrous ending I had seen our own.«

»Thereafter, we kept away from the abominable food, though the desire for it had entered into our blood. Yet our drear punishment was upon us for, day by day, with monstrous rapidity, the fungoid growth took hold of our poor bodies. Nothing we could do would check it materially, and so – and so – we who had been humans became ... Well, it matters less each day. Only – only, we had been man and maid!

»And day by day the fight is more dreadful, to withstand the hunger – lust for the terrible lichen.«

»A week ago, we ate the last of the biscuits, and since that time, I have caught three fish. I was out here fishing tonight when your schooner drifted upon me out of the mist. I hailed you. You know the rest, and may God, out of His great heart, bless you for your goodness to a – a couple of poor outcast souls.«

»There was the dip of an oar – another. Then the voice came again, and for the last time, sounding through the slight surrounding mist, it was ghostly and mournful.

»God bless you! Good-bye!«

»Good-bye«, we shouted together hoarsely, our hearts full of many emotions.«

»I glanced about me. I became aware that the dawn was upon us.«

»The sun flung a stray beam across the hidden sea; pierced the mist dully, and lit up the receding boat with a gloomy fire. Indistinctly, I saw something nodding between the oars. I thought of a sponge – a great, gray nodding sponge … The oars continued to ply. They were gray – as was the boat – and my eyes searched a moment vainly for the conjunction of hand and oar. My gaze flashed back to the – head.

It nodded forward as the oars went backward for the stroke. Then, the oars were dipped, the boat shot out of the patch of light, and the – the thing went nodding into the mist.

THE PHANTOM REGIMENT OF KILLIECRANKIE
by Elliott O'Donnell (1911)

Many are the stories that have from time to time been circulated with regard to the haunting of the pass of Killiecrankie by phantom soldiers, but I do not think there is any stranger story than that related to me, some years ago, by a lady who declared she had actually witnessed the phenomenon. Her account of it I shall reproduce as far as possible in her own words:

Let me commence by stating that I am not a spiritualist, and that I have the greatest possible aversion to convoking the earthbound souls of the dead. Neither do I lay any claim to mediumistic powers (indeed, I have always regarded the term 'medium' with the gravest suspicion). I am, on the contrary, a plain, practical, matter-of-fact woman, and with the exception of this one occasion, I have never witnessed any psychic phenomena.

The incident I am about to relate took place in the autumn before last. I was on a cycle tour in Scotland, and, making Pitlochry my temporary headquarters, rode over one evening to view the historic pass of Killiecrankie. It was late when I arrived there, and the western sky was one great splash of crimson and gold

– such vivid coloring I had never seen before and have never seen since.

Indeed, I was so entranced by the sublimity of the spectacle that I perched myself on a rock at the foot of one of the great cliffs that form the walls of the pass. And, throwing my head back, I imagined myself in fairyland. Lost, thus, in a delicious luxury, I paid no heed to the time, nor did I think of stirring, until the dark shadows of the night fell across my face.

I then started up in a panic and was about to pedal off in a hot haste, when a strange notion suddenly seized me: I had a latchkey, plenty of sandwiches, and a warm cape. Why should I not camp out there till early morning – I had long yearned to spend a night in the open, now was my opportunity.

The idea was no sooner conceived than put into operation. Selecting the most comfortable-looking boulder I could see, I scrambled on to the top of it and, with my cloak drawn tightly over my back and shoulders, commenced my vigil. The cold mountain air, sweet with the perfume of gorse and heather, intoxicated me, and I gradually sank into a heavenly torpor, from which I was abruptly aroused by a dull boom that I at once associated with distant musketry.

All was then still, still as the grave, and, on glancing at the watch I wore strapped to my wrist, I saw it was two o'clock. A species of nervous dread now laid hold of me, and a thousand and one vague fancies, all the more distressing because of their vagueness, oppressed and disconcerted me. Moreover, I was impressed for the first time with the extraordinary solitude – solitude that seemed to belong to a period far other than the present and, as I glanced around at the solitary pines and gleaming boulders, I more than half expected to see the wild, ferocious face of some robber chief – some fierce yet fascinating hero of Sir Walter Scott's – peering at me from behind them.

This feeling at length became so acute that, in a panic of fear – ridiculous, puerile fear, I forcibly withdrew my gaze and concentrated it abstractedly on the ground at my feet.

I then listened, and in the rustling of a leaf, the humming of some night insect, the whizzing of a bat and the whispering of the wind as it moaned softly past me, I fancied – nay, I felt sure I detected something that was not ordinary. I blew my nose and had barely ceased marveling at the loudness of its reverberations before the piercing, ghoulish shriek of an owl sent the blood in torrents to my heart. I then laughed, and my blood froze as I heard a chorus of what I tried to persuade myself could only be echoes, proceeding from every crag and rock in the valley.

For some seconds after this, I sat still, hardly daring to breathe, and pretending to be extremely angry with myself for being such a fool. With a stupendous effort, I turned my attention to the most material of things. One of the skirt buttons on my hip – they were much in vogue then – being loose, I endeavored to occupy myself in tightening it, and when I could no longer derive any employment from that, I set to work on my shoes, and tied knots in the laces, merely to enjoy the task of untying them.

But this, too, ceasing at last to attract me, I was desperately racking my mind for some other device, when there came again the queer, booming noise I had heard before, but which I could now no longer doubt was the report of firearms.

I looked in the direction of the sound – and – my heart almost stopped. Racing towards me – as if not merely for his life, but his soul – came the figure of a Highlander. The wind rustling through his long, disheveled hair blew it completely over his forehead, narrowly missing his eyes, which were fixed ahead of him in a ghastly, agonized stare. He had not a vestige of color, and, in the powerful glow of the moonbeams, his skin shone livid. He ran with huge bounds, and there was something that added to my terror and made me double-aware he was nothing mortal: Each time his feet struck the hard, smooth road, upon which I could well see there was no sign of a stone, there came the sound – the unmistakable sound of the scattering of gravel.

On, on he came, with cyclonic swiftness. His bare sweating elbows pressed into his panting sides; his great, dirty, coarse, hairy fists screwed up in bony bunches in front of him; the foam-flakes thick on his clenched, grinning lips; the blood-drops oozing down his sweating thighs.

It was all real, infernally, hideously real, even to the most minute details: the flying up and down of his kilt, sporran, and swordless scabbard; the bursting of the seam of his coat, near the shoulder; and the absence of one of his clumsy shoe-buckles.

I tried hard to shut my eyes, but was compelled to keep them open and follow his every movement as, darting past me, he left the roadway and, leaping several of the smaller obstacles that barred his way, finally disappeared behind some of the bigger boulders. I then heard the loud rat-tat of drums, accompanied by the shrill voices of fifes and flutes, and at the farther end of the pass, their arms glittering brightly in the silvery moonbeams, appeared a regiment of scarlet-clad soldiers.

At the head rode a mounted officer, after him came the band, and then, four abreast, a long line of warriors; in their center two ensigns, and on their flanks, officers and non-commissioned officers with swords and pikes; more mounted men bringing up the rear.

On they came, the fifes and flutes ringing out with a weird clarity in the hushed mountain air. I could hear the ground vibrate, the gravel crunch and scatter, as they steadily and mechanically advanced – tall men, enormously tall men, with set, white faces and livid eyes.

Every instant I expected they would see me, and I became sick with terror at the thought of meeting all those pale, flashing eyes. But from this, I was happily saved; no one appeared to notice me, and they all passed me by without as much as a twist or turn of the head, their feet keeping time to one everlasting and monotonous tramp, tramp, tramp. I got up and watched until the last of them had turned the bend of the pass, and the sheen of his weapons and trappings could no longer be seen; then I remounted my boulder and wondered if anything further would happen.

It was now half past two, and blended with the moonbeams was a peculiar whiteness that rendered the whole aspect of my surroundings indescribably dreary and ghostly. Feeling cold and hungry, I set to work on my beef sandwiches and was religiously separating the fat from the lean, for I am one of those foolish people who detest fat, when a loud rustling made me look up.

Confronting me, on the opposite side of the road, was a tree, an ash, and to my surprise, despite the fact that the breeze had fallen and there was scarcely a breath of wind, the tree swayed violently to and fro, while there proceeded from it the most dreadful moanings and groanings. I was so terrified that I caught hold of my bicycle and tried to mount, but I was obliged to desist as I had not a particle of strength in my limbs.

Then, to assure myself that the moving of the tree was not an illusion, I rubbed my eyes, pinched myself, and called aloud, but it made no difference – the rustling, bending, and tossing still continued.

Summing up courage, I stepped into the road to get a closer view, when, to my horror, my feet kicked against something, and, on looking down, I perceived the body of an English soldier, with a ghastly wound in his chest. I gazed around, and there, on all sides of me, from one end of the valley to the other, lay dozens of bodies – bodies of men and horses – Highlanders and English, white-cheeked, lurid eyes, and bloody-browed – a hotch-potch of livid, gory awfulness.

Here was the writhing, wriggling figure of an officer with half his face shot away; and there a horse with no head; and there – but I cannot dwell on such horrors, the very memory of which makes me feel sick and faint. The air, that beautiful, fresh mountain air, resounded with their moanings and groanings and reeked with the smell of their blood.

As I stood rooted to the ground with horror, not knowing which way to look or turn, I suddenly saw drop from the ash the form of a woman, a Highland girl, with bold, handsome features, raven black hair, and the whitest of arms and feet.

In one hand, she carried a wicker basket, and in the other a knife – a broad-bladed, sharp-edged, horn-handled knife. A gleam of avarice and cruelty came into her large, dark eyes, and wandering around her, they rested on the rich facings of the English officers' uniforms. I knew what was in her mind, and – forgetting she was but a ghost – that they were all ghosts – I moved heaven and earth to stop her.

I could not. Making straight for a wounded officer that lay moaning piteously on the ground, some ten feet away from me, she spurned with her slender, graceful feet the bodies of the dead and dying English that came in her way. Then, snatching the officer's sword and pistol from him, she knelt down and, with a look of devilish glee in her glorious eyes, calmly plunged her knife into his heart, working the blade backwards and forwards to assure herself she had made a thorough job of it. Anything more hellish I could not have imagined, and yet it fascinated me – the girl was so fair, so wickedly fair and shapely. In her act of cruelty, she spoiled her victim of his rings, epaulets, buttons, and gold lacing and, having placed them in her basket, proceeded elsewhere.

In some cases, unable to remove the rings easily, she chopped off the fingers and popped them, just as they were, into her basket. Neither was her mode of dispatch always the same, for while she put some men out of their misery in the manner I have described, she cut the throats of others with as great a nonchalance as if she had been killing fowls, while others again she settled with the butt-ends of their guns or pistols. In all, she murdered a full half-score and was decamping with her booty when her gloating eyes suddenly encountered mine, and with a shrill scream of rage, she rushed towards me. I was an easy victim for strain and prey. No matter how tried, I could not move an inch. Raising her flashing blade high over her head, and with an expression of fiendish glee in her staring eyes, she made ready to strike me.

This was the climax. My overstrained nerves could stand no more, and when the blow had time to descend, I pitched heavily forward and fell at her feet. When I recovered, every phantom had vanished, and the pass glowed with all the cheerful freshness of the early morning sun. Not a whit the worse for my venture, I cycled swiftly home and ate as only one can eat who has spent the night amid the banks and braes of bonnie Scotland.